WHERE MOONBEAMS DANCE

Hannah Maxwell's gambler husband Brian dies suddenly from a brain haemorrhage, leaving her struggling to bring up her three children amidst a mountain of debt. Then a distant relative bequeaths to her a tidy sum, and the tenancy of a Highland croft. A stranger to the countryside, Hannah is determined to make a new life for her family — but brooding Ross Hunter, the estate manager, is less than welcoming. Yet Hannah finds herself increasingly drawn to him, and his help at the croft becomes indispensable . . .

RENA GEORGE

WHERE MOONBEAMS DANCE

Complete and Unabridged

LINFORD
Leicester

First published in Great Britain in 2013

First Linford Edition
published 2014

A catalogue record for this book is available
from the British Library.

ISBN 978–1–4448–2116–1

Published by
F. A. Thorpe (Publishing)
Anstey, Leicestershire

Set by Words & Graphics Ltd.
Anstey, Leicestershire
Printed and bound in Great Britain by
T. J. International Ltd., Padstow, Cornwall

This book is printed on acid-free paper

1

Hannah had been putting off this moment for the past two days, but she knew she couldn't ignore the letters forever. It wasn't as though she didn't know what they contained. For an intelligent woman, she was behaving completely irrationally.

She glanced at the drawer where the two white envelopes nestled amongst the tea towels, and felt the leaden sickness in the pit of her stomach. This time last year they'd been a normal family. Money was tight, but when wasn't it? She and Brian weren't exactly ecstatically happy together, but they got along.

Hannah's parents had never approved of her marrying Brian. She could still hear her mother's voice: 'It's not that he's still only a shop assistant, Hannah. It's the fact that he doesn't seem to have any ambition to better himself.'

Hannah had been furious. 'What's

wrong with being a shop assistant?'

Peggy Gilmore had sighed. 'Nothing, love, but a shop assistant's wages won't support a family . . . well, not in any comfortable way. Your dad and I only want to see you enjoying your young life, and not be scrimping for necessities as we always had to.'

Hannah caught the glint of tears in her mother's eyes and she touched her shoulder. 'I know you and Dad mean well, but I really do love Brian.' And she did . . . well, in those days anyway. But after Robbie came along, things changed.

Hannah had always been good at sewing, and when the opportunity of working for a Glasgow kilt-maker came along, Peggy had been more than happy to look after her little grandson. Eager to learn new skills, Hannah had watched how the other women worked, studied how they cut the rich tartan fabrics, and stitched each pleat into place. In less than a year she had become an accomplished kilt-maker, and friends were asking if she'd make kilts for them at home. She knew her employers would have frowned on it, but she wasn't stealing any of their customers. The extra cash meant they could put down a deposit on a house.

Brian hadn't been able to see the point of buying property when they had a perfectly adequate council house, but Hannah wanted better for her family. Glancing down at the two official envelopes in her hand, she wondered now if he'd been right all along. She put the letters on the table and sat staring at them.

How had it all come to this? Her mind drifted back over the years. When Jamie came along, two years after Robbie, they'd moved to this small three-bedroom end-of-terrace home on the new estate. Four years later, Holly had been born. Brian was spending more and more time in the pub, and when Hannah pointed out that they couldn't afford for him to go out drinking so much, he insisted he could make a pint last all evening. Sometimes he came back in high spirits, and life would be good for a few weeks. Then the black moods would return, and he'd snap at her attempts to discover what was wrong.

'You let Brian get away with murder, you know that, Hannah, don't you?' It was a frequent complaint when her mother visited. 'You're holding down a full-time job, and then coming home to do all this extra work. And what does Brian do?' This was inevitably accompanied by some gesture of exasperation. 'He spends it all in the pub, that's what.'

Hannah would bite her lip and say nothing. Brian was her husband, and she wouldn't criticise him behind his back — not even to her mother. She sighed and began folding away the bolt of tartan she'd ordered for her next commission, but her mind kept drifting back to her mother's warnings. She put her hand on the small of her back and stretched. She could still hear her raised voice; the defiant words.

'Brian's working too, you know. You

make it sound as though he's out every night spending my wages.'

Peggy had never heard her daughter utter a bad word against Brian. But surely she knew about his gambling? It was all going to end in tears. Alec told her often enough not to get involved. She knew he was right, but this was Hannah's life, and there were the three little ones to think about.

The real blow came when Brian lost his job. He'd said it was redundancy . . . last in, first out. But Hannah had never seen any redundancy money. The DIY chain store had never been a generous payer. Even with her wages, and the extra she earned from the home commissions, they'd just about managed to scrape by most months. Hannah shook her head, remembering.

'It's not as bad as you're thinking,' Brian had said coaxingly. 'I'll get another job . . . a better one.'

She'd cried herself to sleep that night. That was when she finally accepted that their marriage was over.

She wouldn't leave, of course. She had Robbie, Jamie and little Holly to think about. Even a bad father was better than no dad at all. And she couldn't deny that Brian loved his children. But he didn't find another job, and the frustration of that turned him right back to gambling.

The letter from the building society brought more dismay. Brian had fallen behind with the mortgage repayments. Looking back now, Hannah realised she should have taken more responsibility over the family finances, but she'd been too busy trying to boost her husband's ego. He'd taken it badly when he'd lost his job. It would have been like taking his manhood away completely if she'd suddenly suggested that she should handle the family money.

And then it happened! It was six months ago now, but the scene still played out in her mind like horrific newsreel film on a never-ending loop. Saturday morning, and her mum and dad had called to take the children out for the day. She'd been working in the kitchen and Brian was upstairs having a shower. Suddenly, there was an almighty thud. Hannah stopped, listening.

'Are you all right, Brian?' she called up the stairs, thinking he'd managed to pull the loose shower rail down. There was no reply.

She called again. 'Brian . . . ?'

Her heart was pounding as she raced up the stairs. The bathroom door was ajar. She could hear the water splashing into the bath. She pushed the door open.

'Brian?'

But the name froze on her lips. Her husband was splayed across the bath, the shower water still drumming down on his face. He wasn't moving.

'Oh my God, Brian!' She sprang forward to help him up, and then stumbled back, her eyes wide with horror. She had no recollection of screaming his name, of tearing downstairs to phone for help, of opening the front door as their neighbour, Laura, rushed in. She had a hazy memory of Laura asking for her mobile phone to ring for an ambulance. It was there within minutes. But it was already too late. Brian was dead. The doctors later told her it had been a brain haemorrhage, and that Brian wouldn't have known a thing about it.

She stared down at the tartan fabric she had been folding and a tear trickled down her cheek. Their marriage hadn't turned out to be the love match Hannah had hoped for, but she still missed him. She swiped at the tears as she heard her mother's quick rap on the back door before she came into the kitchen.

'You've been crying,' Peggy said accusingly. 'Please tell me it's not more bad news.'

Hannah forced a smile and shook her head. 'No, just me being silly.'

'You might be many things, my darling, but silly isn't one of them. What's wrong?'

Peggy's hand suddenly went to her throat.

'It's not the children, is it?'

Hannah put up a hand and shook her head. 'They're all fine, Mum. If anything, they've coped with their father's death better than I have.' She looked up and met her mother's blue eyes. 'I've got you and Dad to thank for that. You've sheltered them from most of the trauma. You don't know how thankful I am that they were with you when . . . ' Her voice faltered. ' . . . when it happened.'

'Oh, Hannah.' Peggy Gilmore came round the table to give her daughter a hug. 'I know it's hard, but for the children's sake you must try to move on.'

Hannah's eyes slid to the letters. She still couldn't quite believe what Brian had done to his family. How could he have been so irresponsible as to stop paying the mortgage? 'It's not that, Mum,' she said shakily. She pointed. 'It's them.' Peggy raised an eyebrow. 'Brian got behind with the mortgage re-payments,' she said flatly.

'No.' Peggy sank onto a chair. 'How bad is it?'

Hannah tried to steady her voice. 'That's a repossession notice.'

She heard her mother's sharp intake of breath. Peggy spoke gently. 'They can't just take your house, love. They have to give you notice. Even the most hard-hearted building society can't turn a young family out into the street.'

'It's not the first letter,' Hannah said quietly. 'That one arrived soon after . . . soon after I lost Brian.'

Peggy gasped. 'Why didn't you tell us?'

'I thought at first I could handle it, make up the missed payments some-how, but . . . ' She shrugged. 'There just wasn't enough money coming in.'

'You should have come to us.'

Hannah's shoulders lifted in a hope-less shrug. 'It's £5000, Mum. You and Dad don't have that kind of money. And besides, I couldn't ask you.'

Peggy released a long, shuddering sigh. It was true. She and Alec were

10

already struggling to make ends meet. 'Have you spoken to the building society?'

Hannah ran her fingers through her hair. 'They want the full amount, Mum.' She swallowed. 'They just want their money.'

Peggy's eyes narrowed. 'I suppose if the worst happens, and the building society does sell the house, there will be some money left over. At least that should give you a cushion in the meantime.'

Hannah shook her head. 'The house is worth less now than what we paid for it ten years ago. It' called negative equity.' She looked up and met her mother's eyes. 'So you see . . . ' She gave a hopeless shrug. 'There is no money.'

For a few moments they sat in silence, both staring at the unopened letters. Then Peggy shook her head.

'I don't understand. Brian was un-employed. He must have been receiving benefits to pay the mortgage. What was he doing with the money?'

Hannah sighed. 'Brian was a gambler. Need I say more?'

Peggy stared at her daughter. She was speechless.

Hannah cleared her throat. 'Losing his job was a big blow to Brian, and not just because of the money — although we obviously missed that. It destroyed his self-esteem.'

Peggy's eyebrows lifted again, but Hannah ignored her and carried on. 'He was always worried about not being able to provide for his family, Mum. That's how the gambling started. He put money on a horse and it won, so he backed another . . . and then another . . . and so it went on.' She paused. 'At first he was on a winning streak, but of course that didn't last. Eventually he was losing money we didn't have. He tried to borrow, but things just got out of hand.'

Peggy leaned forward, her eyes anxious. 'Couldn't you have intervened somehow, Hannah?'

'How could I, when Brian refused to talk to me? I'd no idea how bad it had all got.' She raked her fingers through her hair again. It was a gesture Peggy noticed her daughter doing a lot recently. 'I wouldn't be surprised if all this worry had something to do with his brain haemorrhage,' Hannah said wearily.

Peggy reached across the table and squeezed her daughter's hand. 'I'm so sorry, love. You should have told me. But your dad and I won't see you and our grandchildren put out onto the street. You must all move in with us . . . at least until you've been allocated a council house.'

'Thanks, Mum, but you only have one spare room. We'd never all manage to squeeze in there.'

'You let us worry about that,' Peggy said, patting Hannah's hand. She nodded towards the unopened letters. 'How long have they given you?'

Hannah bit her lip. 'I've been too scared to open them.'

'Well do it now,' her mother said firmly. 'Let's know the worst.'

Hannah's hand shook as she reached for the now-familiar building society envelope. Peggy watched her daughter's eyes flick over the page before the letter dropped from her fingers. 'The 30th of the month,' Hannah stammered. 'They want us out by the end of the month.'

'But that's just three weeks!' Peggy's eyes were wide. 'We have to work something out here.' Her gaze fell on the second envelope. 'What about that one?' She picked it up and examined it. 'There's a Glasgow solicitor's name on the back.'

Hannah frowned. 'Just leave it. It's obviously something to do with the building society. I can't face any more shocks today, Mum.'

'Ignoring it is not the answer, love,' Peggy said firmly. 'Best get it all over with.'

She offered the envelope across, but Hannah shook her head. 'You do it.' She got up, turning to plug in the kettle.

She couldn't bear to watch her mother's face as she read what was certain to be more bad news. Hannah heard the letter being ripped open — and then her mother's gasp. She swung round, staring. 'For heaven's sake, Mum. Just tell me.' She was steeling herself for the worst. Had Brian also run up a string of debts she knew nothing about? *Please don't let it be that*, she thought.

Peggy's hand had gone to her throat. She looked up and met Hannah's frantic stare, then held out the letter. 'I think you should read this for yourself,' she said, her voice jerky.

Hannah's eyes widened. 'If it's that bad, I don't think I want to read it.'

'I think you'd better,' her mother said quietly.

Hannah took the letter, her eyes scanning the words. 'This has to be a mistake.' She looked up. 'Someone is playing a trick . . . a cruel trick.'

'Well it looks official enough to me,' Peggy said, an incredulous smile beginning to spread across her face.

'But it says here that I've inherited a croft up in the Highlands. That can't be right.' Hannah read the letter again, more slowly this time. 'It says that some relation of Brian's has died and left the property to him.' She swallowed the lump in her throat. 'It seems that as his widow, the property now comes to me.'

Peggy clasped her hands, her eyes shining. 'It's the miracle you've been praying for.'

Hannah held up a hand. 'Slow down, Mum. Let's not count our chickens just yet. This all seems too good to be true. There must be a catch.'

'Or maybe it's time something nice happened for you and the kids.' Peggy's mind was working overtime. 'These old Highland cottages are always in demand. You could make enough from the sale to sort out all your money problems . . . and then some.'

Hannah chewed her lip. 'Do you think so?'

'Ring him,' Peggy said, waggling a finger excitedly at the letter. 'There's a number, look. Ring the solicitor.'

Hannah glanced back down at the letter. 'He suggests I should visit his office tomorrow at ten.' She bit her lip again, her mind working. 'What d'you think? Should I go?'

Her mother nodded. 'Well of course you should. Would you like me to come with you?'

For the first time in weeks, Hannah smiled. 'No thank you, Mum. I think I need to do this by myself.'

2

Hannah's heart was pounding as she sat in the reception area of the solicitor's office. Her appointment was for ten, and she was early. The plump middle-aged secretary who had greeted her sat behind her desk, busily tapping into a computer. Every now and again she glanced up, offering an encouraging smile.

Hannah tried to calm her nerves as she watched the hands move on the old wooden wall clock. She took a deep breath. Why was she so anxious? The letter was quite clear. It was good news. She should be looking forward to hearing what this man had to tell her.

A buzzer rang, and Hannah jumped. The secretary stood up, smiling. 'Mr Campbell's ready for you now, Mrs Maxwell. This way, please.'

Hannah followed the woman along a

corridor and swallowed as she stopped at a door and gave a quick knock. She opened it without waiting for a response and ushered Hannah in.

A small, round man, with a fringe of white hair and a pair of keen grey eyes behind wire-rimmed spectacles, came forward with his hand outstretched. 'I'm Andrew Campbell, Mrs Maxwell.' He indicated a chair. 'Please have a seat.'

Hannah sat down. The solicitor straightened his spectacles.

'Now, let's see . . . ' He began flicking through the documents in front of him, and then suddenly looked up at Hannah. 'Do you know anything about running a croft, Mrs Maxwell?'

Hannah sat forward. 'So it does come to me, then?' She hesitated. 'I mean, Mrs Sutherland was my late husband's aunt. I never actually met her.'

'Oh, it certainly does . . . if you want it, that is.'

Want it? Why would she not want it? A bolt of excitement shot through her.

They weren't destitute! Brian had provided for them after all — even if it was in a way that none of them could ever have imagined. She lifted her chin, squaring her shoulders.

'I'll probably sell the property. I hope you can advise me there, Mr Campbell.'

The solicitor looked up from his papers, and his brow wrinkled. 'I think you've got the wrong end of the stick, Mrs Maxwell. Your husband's aunt didn't own the croft. She only held the tenancy. That is what she bequeathed to your late husband, which now of course passes on to you.'

Hannah pressed her fingertips to her temples and shook her head. 'I don't understand. You mean I haven't been left a croft house?'

The solicitor sank back into his chair. 'Let me explain. The legislation governing these things is very firm. An organisation now known as the Crofting Commission was set up many years ago to protect these Highland crofts. It administers and regulates crofting and keeps all these matters under review.'

Hannah's heart sank. 'So the property isn't mine after all?' She couldn't keep the catch out of her voice.

Andrew Campbell shook his head. 'I'm sorry. I thought you knew the situation.'

Hannah stared at him in dismay. Nothing had changed. All she was being given was the chance to rent this place. She could do that on a council estate, much nearer home.

'These tenancies are very sought after, you know,' the solicitor continued. 'And I understand that Lanrig is especially desirable.' He studied Hannah's face for a moment, and when she didn't reply he went on. 'The croft is on the Corrieglen Estate, so the laird, Sir John Macleod, is the actual owner. Even so, he still needs permission from the commission to actually do anything with it. But that's a good thing, because it means that the estate is responsible for the upkeep of the property.' He looked down, flicking through his papers again. 'Quite a lot of work has been done on the property since your husband's relative died. The croft house is comfortable and there are a couple of good, manageable fields to work. And as far as I can see it is ready to move into.'

Hannah stared at him in disbelief. 'You do realise that I know nothing about farming, and even less about this crofting business?

Mr Campbell smiled. 'This is the Highlands, Mrs Maxwell. People look out for each other up there.'

Hannah tried to smile, but she couldn't wipe the disappointment from her eyes. The old man's heart went out to her. This wasn't at all what she had been expecting. She probably had a young family to bring up on her own now that her husband had died. He studied her for a second, taking in the alert blue eyes and the mass of dark hair curling on her shoulders. The green suit she wore was newly pressed, but even he could see it was far from new.

She probably had money worries, yet there was something about those intelligent eyes and that proud tilt of her head that made him smile. He cleared his throat.

'There is a little money too, of course.' He checked his papers once more. 'Mrs Sutherland left you £15,000.'

Hannah gasped. '£15,000? You mean I get £15,000 even if I don't take on this tenancy?' Her knees where shaking.

'That's correct,' Andrew Campbell said, looking up and smiling at her shocked expression.

'But that's wonderful.' Hannah jumped up. A hundred ideas were racing through her mind. She could use this windfall to pay off the mortgage arrears. *This* was the real bequest. She controlled an urge to rush round the huge desk and hug the man. He was addressing her again.

'It would certainly help with the removal costs, if you did decide to take on the tenancy.'

'What?'

The old solicitor was watching her.

She frowned. The delirium was beginning to fade. £15,000 was like a fortune to her right now. It would certainly ease her immediate financial problems, but she could see that it was no long-term answer. The mortgage was still more than she could afford.

The solicitor had risen from his chair. 'You don't have to decide anything now. Take a bit of time to think about it. Talk it over with your family. There's no immediate hurry.'

But there was. Three weeks from now they would be homeless! Could this croft possibly be a viable solution? What would Robbie, Jamie, and Holly make of it? Would they see it as a great adventure? Perhaps that was what it was — a huge adventure.

She was picturing her parents' faces if she decided to take the croft. Her mother, especially, would be devastated. Could she do this to them? But she was being given a chance that would change her whole life. A tiny spark of exhilaration was beginning to grow inside her.

Could she really do this?

She turned and offered Andrew Campbell her hand. 'Thank you, you've been very kind.'

The solicitor took both her hands in his. 'Not at all my dear,' he said. 'Just let me know what you decide.'

Hannah's head was in a spin as she sat on the bus going home. She'd certainly been given something to think about. As she saw it, there were two options open to her. She could turn her back on the whole croft tenancy business, as her mother would no doubt want, or she could take her courage in her hands and move her family to the Highlands.

Her heart was beginning to flutter in a not unpleasant way. Could she really become a crofter? One thing was certain: her old life had ended. Suddenly she was no longer afraid of the building society repossessing their home. They could have it. She had choices now.

Her decision was made even before

she reached her destination. They were going to the Highlands!

As she walked from the bus stop, Hannah called in at the supermarket and bought the ingredients for the children's favourite supper. They would think it was a celebration.

The boys' eyes lit up when the dish came out of the oven. 'Macaroni cheese!' Robbie cheered.

'Thanks, Mum. We haven't had this for ages,' Jamie said, sliding onto his chair.

Holly's attention was on the apple pie cooling on the worktop. 'Yummy.' She licked her lips. 'Can I have lots and lots of custard?'

Hannah ruffled her daughter's mop of copper curls. 'As much as you like, my darling,' she laughed. She saw the boys exchange a look and immediately felt guilty. She hadn't spoiled them like this in ages. The meal was simple enough, but she'd taken care over it. Perhaps that was what they missed.

She sat down with them, watching as

they tucked into their meal, and tried to imagine them all sitting around a big farmhouse table in Lanrig. If they lived in a croft they would be able to play outside after supper. It wasn't safe for them to do that on the estate; the roads were far too busy.

Hannah rehearsed how she would broach the subject with them as she tidied up after the meal. Could she win them over? She stacked the last of the plates to drain, then wiped her hands on her apron. 'Can you three come through for a minute?' she called from the kitchen.

'But we're all watching *Blue Peter*, Mum,' Jamie whined.

Hannah stuck her head round the door and smiled. The three of them were cross-legged on the floor, watching the presenter make some cardboard masterpiece from silver paper and toilet roll tubes. 'As soon as it's finished then,' she conceded. The three little heads nodded, their eyes never leaving the screen. Hannah joined them, more amused by their intent expressions than what they were watching. When the programme finished, Robbie leapt up and switched off the television.

Then, with the children gathered around her feet, Hannah told them about the croft.

'Would we have to leave school?' Jamie's eyes were unsure.

Hannah nodded. 'Well, yes, but you would have a lovely new school.'

'Can my friend Millie come with us . . . and Jasmine?' Holly ventured hopefully.

Hannah patted her daughter's head. 'I don't think so, darling. Your friends will want to stay here, with their own mummies.'

'Then I'm not going,' Holly declared, her bottom lip sticking out determinedly.

'Well, maybe they could come and visit us during the holidays. What do you say, sweetheart?'

But Holly still wasn't convinced. Hannah tried again.

'There are lots of fields and animals up in the Highlands. We could all have a really good time.' She turned to Robbie. 'What do you think, Robbie?'

'I think it's rubbish!' he shouted, scrambling up and stamping his feet. 'And I'm not going!' They all stared after him as he stomped out of the room.

'Why do we have to move?' Jamie asked tearfully. 'All our friends are here.'

'Will Grannie and Gramps come with us?' Holly fixed Hannah with wide blue eyes.

Hannah swallowed. She hadn't handled this well — and she still had to break the news to her parents. She got down on her knees and put her arms around Jamie and Holly. 'Tell you what. Let's go online. We might find a picture of the croft.' Out of the corner of her eye she saw Robbie sidle back into the room. She booted up the laptop.

'Google Earth, Mummy,' Jamie said, a tinge of excitement now in his voice.

Why hadn't she thought of doing this

earlier? But then the croft might be so remote that it wasn't on the system.

The solicitor had mentioned Corrieglen Estate. She typed it in.

'It's found something . . . look.' Jamie was definitely getting excited. Even Holly was showing an interest. And behind her, Hannah could sense Robbie moving closer.

A patchwork of green fields began to emerge. Hannah zoomed in.

'There . . . look, Mummy! There it is.' Jamie pointed at the screen. 'Lanrig.'

It was a bird's eye view. They could see an L-shaped rooftop and another couple of buildings that looked like barns or sheds. There was a small walled garden, surrounded by fields of crops.

'Are those cows?' Robbie had appeared behind them. 'And some sheep . . . look.'

Hannah smiled, pointing. 'I think that's a river down there as well.'

'Cool,' Jamie said.

She glanced round at the three animated faces. 'It doesn't look too bad, does it?'

'Can we really stay there, Mummy?' Holly asked.

Hannah nodded and bit her lip. 'If you all agree.'

Jamie and Holly clapped their hands.

'But I'm coming back if I don't like it,' Robbie warned.

Hannah ruffled his hair. 'We'll have to see about that.'

She knew it wouldn't be easy explaining her decision to her mother, but now that she had the children on her side it might not be so bad.

She was wrong.

'For heaven's sake, Hannah, what do you know about running a farm?' Peggy Gilmore rounded on her daughter.

'It's a croft, Mum. And I can learn.'

'It's ridiculous. You'd be miles from anywhere. Do you want the children to grow up bleating like sheep?'

Hannah sighed. 'I don't exactly have many options.'

'Well of course you do.' Peggy's voice was exasperated. 'You'll be eligible for a council house, and until then you could all come and stay with us. Dad and I would love to have you.'

'It's very kind of you, Mum, but you know it's not practical.'

'Nonsense. The children could go into our spare room and you could have the sofa.'

'How is that a solution? You and Dad live miles away. The children would still have to change schools. Their lives would still be disrupted.'

But Peggy wasn't giving up. 'What about that bequest you mentioned? Surely you could use that to pay off the mortgage arrears?'

Hannah bit her lip, trying to stay calm. Did her mother think she wasn't fully aware of all these things? She kept her voice steady. 'Even if I managed to pay off the arrears, there's no way I could afford the mortgage payments on my own. I have thought it all through, Mum.'

'But a croft house, Hannah . . . and away up there in the middle of nowhere. You wouldn't know a soul.'

'I'll make new friends . . . we all will. I hear the Highland schools are very good.'

Peggy released a gasp of exasperation. 'Couldn't you go back to that solicitor, talk to him, make him realise that you would be far better off selling the place?'

'But it's not mine to sell. I've explained it all, Mum. Brian's aunt Lizzie has only left the *tenancy* of the croft. It's actually owned by the Corrieglen Estate.' She raked her fingers through her hair. 'Even the laird can't sell it without permission from this commission thing. It's the law.'

'But if you're only renting it, then what's the point?'

Hannah put her arms around her mother. 'Oh, Mum. Can't you just be happy for us? We'll all miss each other, but Corrieglen isn't a million miles away. You and Dad can come up whenever you like.'

Peggy turned away, not wanting Hannah to see the unexpected tears.

She swallowed back the emotion. 'You're right, love. I'm being selfish,' she stammered. 'This would be a new start for all of you.' She bit her lip and managed a weak smile. 'My daughter . . . the crofter? I'll believe it when I see it.'

3

Hannah loved the outdoors. Before the children came along she and Brian would often take the train from Glasgow to Balloch, and spend the day walking in the hills around Loch Lomond. But they'd never gone as far north as Inverness, let alone Corrieglen, which was a good fifty miles beyond. She'd checked the map before setting out. It was a long way north.

She'd bought a magazine from the kiosk at the railway station, but it lay unread in her bag. So much dramatic scenery was flashing past the carriage window that she needed no further distraction. It was early September, but the trees were still heavy with leaf. Spikey conifers and tall, dramatic Scots pines dominated the landscape, their heads disappearing into the white, clingy mist.

Three and a half hours after leaving Queen Street Station, Hannah stepped out onto the platform at Inverness. She took a deep breath, enjoying the sensation of the sharp, clean air filling her lungs. She could have been on top of a mountain in Switzerland.

There was an hour to kill before her connection to Corrieglen. Not enough time to explore, but at least she could venture out of the station and find a cafe. She'd vaguely imagined Inverness to be some kind of rural backwater, where all the men wore kilts and tweed jackets and fresh-faced women hurried along, shopping baskets laden with local produce. So the stream of mid-morning traffic outside the station made her gasp, but it didn't detract from the pleasure of just being there. Passers-by nodded and smiled at her as she walked. In Glasgow most of the busy city commuters ignored each other. She liked the feel of this friendly new place.

Then she really did spot a man in a

kilt. He was sprinting across the road to beat the changing traffic lights. It made her smile, for it sowed the seeds of an idea — something she would enjoy giving a lot more thought to on the journey home.

The cafe she found was only five minutes from the station, but Hannah didn't dawdle over the tea and toasted muffins for fear of missing her connection north.

The platform was at the far end of the station, and her train was already waiting when she arrived. It was smaller, and certainly a lot older, than the one she'd just travelled on from Glasgow. She settled into her seat, glancing around the carriage. The only other passenger was a neat, silver-haired woman, who smiled at her from across the aisle.

Hannah's heart gave a lurch as the train pulled out of the station, gathering speed as they raced along the side of a loch. How Robbie, Jamie and little Holly would have loved this adventure. She checked the timetable she'd collected from the ticket office in Inverness. Only five stops before Corrieglen. She could feel her heart skip a beat.

'Going far, dear?'

Hannah looked up, unaware the woman had been studying her. 'Emm . . . Corrieglen,' Hannah said.

The stranger laughed. 'You don't look too sure.'

'Oh, I'm sure all right. It's just that . . . well, I've never been here before, so I'm watching the stops.'

'Well you don't have to worry about going past your station, because that's where I'm getting off.' The woman pursed her lips and tilted her head at Hannah. 'If you're not being met, I could offer you a lift at the other end. My Jake's picking me up.'

'That's kind of you, but I am being met.'

The woman raised an eyebrow, encouraging further explanation. Hannah obliged. 'Someone from the Corrieglen Estate is meeting me.'

The woman nodded, and then stretched her hand towards Hannah. 'Maggie Morrison's the name. I run the post office in Corrieglen.' She paused, a finger at her mouth. 'I don't want to sound interfering, but are you planning on staying the night in the village?'

Hannah nodded.

'Well I run a B&B if it's accommodation you'll be needing.'

'Really? I've been wondering if there would be anywhere to stay.'

Maggie smiled. 'Consider yourself booked in for the night, then.'

They got off the train together, Hannah helping her new acquaintance with her bags. 'This will be your taxi,' the woman said, nodding to the tall man walking towards them. 'This young lady will be staying with us tonight, Ross. Make sure you get her back safely.'

The man nodded, no hint of welcome in the serious green eyes. He looked every inch the country squire in his tweed jacket over a thick brown polo-necked jumper. And although his weather-beaten features were not, strictly speaking, handsome, he had a definite presence. He strode forward, offering his hand.

'Ross Hunter,' he said, his brow furrowing. 'I'm the estate manager at Corrieglen.'

Hannah shot her hand out. 'I'm Hannah Maxwell. Pleased to meet you.' They shook hands and he gestured towards a mud-splattered Land Rover. 'Not allergic to dogs, are you?'

Hannah smiled at the Border collie panting in the back of the vehicle, and leaned over to ruffle its fur. At her touch the dog's tail thumped the seat.

'He's lovely. What's his name?'

Ross glanced round and raised a warning eyebrow at the dog. '*Her* name's Tess,' he said. 'And she's a working dog, not a pet.' He started the engine, and they bumped out of the station car park.

It wasn't the welcome Hannah hoped for. She slid a glance at Ross, wondering what he was thinking, as they sped along the country lanes. Had meeting her at the railway station just been an irritating chore he'd had to do? He was making no attempt at conversation, so she turned her attention back to the road.

Ross was surprised by the young woman's silence. He'd been steeling himself for non-stop chatter . . . a barrage of questions. But Hannah Maxwell just sat quietly beside him, watching the passing scenery. She wasn't at all what he had been expecting. For a start, she was much younger than he had anticipated. She didn't look old enough to be the mother of three children, and for a recently widowed woman he couldn't detect the expected air of grief. The one thing he was sure of, though, was that this was no countrywoman. He doubted if she had ever been on a farm in her life, let alone a croft. What would a city woman, never mind a single mother, do with a croft?

He'd already decided that she had only turned up out of curiosity, when she gave a little cough and turned to him. 'Have you worked for the estate for long, Mr Hunter?'

Ross didn't answer immediately and Hannah was about to repeat her question, when he nodded. 'Sir John took me on as a boy, to help the old ghillie. That was twenty years ago. I've been here ever since.'

'Sir John? That'll be the laird?'

Ross nodded again.

'Will I be meeting him today?' Hannah asked.

'Do you want to?'

'No, I mean . . . I just wondered.' The thought of meeting a real-life laird shot a bolt of alarm through her. She gave herself a shake. He was just a man. Why was she being such a wimp?

Ross Hunter kept his eyes on the narrow lane ahead. 'My instructions are to show you round Lanrig, but if you want a sneak preview of the Big House then just take a look to your left.'

Through the trees, in the distance at the end of the far fields, Hannah could

42

make out a large building.

'That's Corrieglen House,' Ross said, swinging the Land Rover to the right. 'Lanrig is just down here.'

They turned onto a rutted track that wound its way downhill. Hannah recognised the terrain. The L-shaped cottage she could see at the bottom was the one they had looked at on her laptop. A wooden crossbar gate at the end of the track stood open. She squinted at the faded peeling letters. *Lanrig.* They drove on, turning into a cobbled yard at the back of the croft house. In front of it, Hannah glimpsed a paddock sweeping down to the river. She gasped. It all felt so familiar.

'It's beautiful,' she said breathlessly.

Ross Hunter frowned. 'I'd take off the rose-coloured specs if I were you, Mrs Maxwell. This place will be hard work. A croft tenancy comes with responsibilities to work and care for the land. It's not like a holiday home, you know.'

His words were stinging. What was

wrong with this man? She rounded on him.

'I was told you Highland people were supposed to be friendly, neighbourly folk. But quite frankly, Mr Hunter, I find your attitude hostile. I may never have run a place like this, but it's only a smallholding after all, and I think I'm quite capable of doing that.' She swallowed, struggling to keep her temper. 'Besides, I haven't even decided if I want this tenancy yet.'

Her outburst had obviously shocked him, for he was staring wide-eyed at her now, and his face had developed an even higher colour. He cleared his throat. 'I've no wish to appear *hostile*' — he emphasised the word — 'Mrs Maxwell, and I apologise if I've been giving that impression.'

'Oh for goodness sake, stop calling me Mrs Maxwell. My name's Hannah.' She paused, squinting up at him. 'And I think we just got off on the wrong foot. How about a truce?' She shot out her hand again. It was a second before he took it, but when he did, there was still no amusement in the green eyes.

'Ross,' he said solemnly. 'And just for the record, I wasn't suggesting that you weren't capable.'

'So you have no prejudice against a woman running a croft?'

He shook his head. 'I can hardly claim that. Lizzie Sutherland ran this place on her own after Seth passed on, and she made a damn good job of it.'

'Lizzie sounds like a hard act to follow.'

Ross nodded. 'You could say that.'

There was another awkward silence and Hannah began to climb out of the vehicle. 'Can I have a look inside?'

Ross reached into his jacket pocket for the keys. 'That's why we're here.'

Hannah slid him a look. This man really was determined not be friendly. He unlocked the back door, pushing it open and allowing Hannah to step inside. She was in a flagstone passage with a kitchen to her left and a big sitting room to the right. She went into the kitchen, her nose twitching. The cottage had a curious smell.

'It's the peat Lizzie used to burn. The smell lingers.'

'I like it,' Hannah said.

She'd expected the interior of the cottage to be dark, but the rooms were flooded with light. Both the kitchen and the reception room had double windows overlooking the front pasture and the river beyond. The kitchen also had a rear window onto the yard. The views to the front were breathtaking and she'd been about to exclaim how beautiful it all was again, when she remembered Ross's reaction the last time she'd done that, so she said nothing. A few threadbare rugs were scattered on the stone floors, but apart from that, Brian's elderly aunt had obviously not bothered much about creature comforts. Hannah put her hand on the kitchen wall.

'It feels old,' she said, turning to Ross.

He nodded, looking around him. 'I

should say a couple of centuries at least. These old croft houses were built to last.'

He followed her as she wandered through the rooms and tried to imagine her living here with her family. She couldn't possibly be considering taking this on by herself. There would be a man somewhere in the background. Women like her didn't stay single for long. With or without a man, she'd have her work cut out if she decided to take the tenancy of Lanrig. There was Jess Guthrie for a start. She wouldn't be giving any new tenant an easy ride, not when she had her mind set on moving her son, Gil, in here. Ross thought about that. Surely the laird would never allow it? Gil Guthrie would run the place into the ground. Lanrig deserved better.

Hannah was back in the kitchen with a tape measure. She'd decided she could just about squeeze her washing machine into this space next to the old sink. The bedrooms upstairs were a bit more cramped than she would have liked, but it was all certainly do-able.

'Are all the electrics working?' She swung round and was surprised to find Ross watching her.

'Everything is working,' he said, coming to stand beside her at the window. They were looking out over the yard. Ross nodded to the far corner. 'There's an old well over there. In the old days that's where Lizzie and Seth got their water.'

Hannah's eyes widened. 'You mean they had to carry buckets of water from out there every time they wanted a cup of tea?'

Ross pursed his lips. 'Pretty much.'

Didn't they have a bathroom . . . or a toilet even? How could they manage?' Hannah was shocked. She thought she saw the trace of a smile on the stern face.

'They had some kind of out-of-doors arrangement,' he said.

Hannah stared out across the yard. Her respect for Lizzie Sutherland was growing by the minute. She pulled her camera from her bag and began taking pictures of the cottage, inside and out. She couldn't wait to share this experience with her family.

Ross was watching her, trying to see the place with Hannah's eyes. More effort should have been put into making it presentable. He should have seen to it himself, but an empty croft house hadn't been his highest priority over the last few months. He had his hands full just making sure the estate business held together. The number of shooting parties Corrieglen attracted these days was dwindling, and the sale of fishing permits certainly wasn't what it used to be. People were tightening their belts, and the estate, like so many others in the Highlands, was feeling the pinch.

Still . . . he should have paid more attention to Lanrig. His glance travelled to the front window, through which he could see the tangle of weeds that used to be Lizzie's handsome rose bed. It wouldn't have taken more than a few hours' hard graft to tidy up the whole garden, yet it hadn't been done. He was annoyed with himself and the irritation showed.

Hannah spun round to face him. 'You don't want me to take on this place, do you, Mr Hunter?'

They were back on stiffly formal terms, which was exactly what he deserved. When he'd first seen her at the railway station with Maggie, he'd thought her to be in her mid-twenties, but now he could see there were tiny lines etched under her eyes. He noticed they were a very dark blue, and at that moment challenging him to respond.

He swallowed. 'My only interest is in finding the right tenant for Lanrig.' Even to his ears his voice sounded curt and dismissive.

'And you don't think I'm that person?' She crossed the room and held out her hands, turning them palms-up. 'Do these look like the hands of an idle woman, Mr Hunter? I've had to work hard all my life . . . ' Her voice faltered.

'And now I have three young children to support on my own.' Her eyes went to the pasture that swept down to the river. 'If I decide to bring my family here, it won't be because I think it will be a holiday.' She tilted her chin and gave him a defiant glare. 'It's true that I know little about crofting, but I'm not stupid. I can learn . . . and I'm no stranger to hard work.'

The outburst took Ross by surprise and for a moment he was stunned into silence. He couldn't think of anything to say, so he just nodded and followed her back outside. She marched ahead of him back to the vehicle and waited, arms folded, while he locked up. Her heart was thudding in her chest. No one had ever made her so angry. All she wanted to do now was to catch the next train back to Inverness. Maybe there was still time to make a connection to Glasgow. This had been a mistake. Why did she even consider coming to this place?

Hannah's outburst had stirred Ross

more than he cared to admit. Could he have misjudged the woman? There was no mistaking the fire in her eyes when she spoke of her children. This was a mother who'd do anything to keep her family together. Maybe he'd been wrong about her. Maybe she wasn't that different from Lizzie. She certainly had spirit — and now she was leaving with the distinct impression that he didn't think she was capable of running the croft on her own.

A picture of Gil Guthrie floated through his mind. If Hannah didn't take the tenancy, then he would be the alternative — and that would be too much of a nightmare to even contemplate.

'Just take me back to the railway station, please. I've seen enough,' Hannah said stiffly as Ross got into the vehicle and slid behind the wheel.

He turned, knowing he should apologise, but the words stuck in his throat. He wasn't used to situations like this. He was out of his depth. 'So you're quitting before you even start?' His voice sounded gruff, even to him.

Hannah swung round, eyes round with fury. 'You more or less told me that I wasn't good enough for your precious Lanrig.'

'I don't recall saying that.'

'Well you certainly gave that impression, with your sideways looks and your scowls, and your raised eyebrows.'

Ross shook his head, frowning. 'Look . . . I . . . emm . . . Well you can't go yet.' She was still staring at him. 'You've made your arrangements with Maggie and . . . well, it wouldn't be right to let her down.' Hannah's eyes widened. 'And besides, you'd never get a connection back to Glasgow at this time of day.'

For a few moments there was silence between them, then Hannah cleared her throat. 'Is that it? Is that all you have to say?'

Ross threw the vehicle into reverse and they began to hurtle back up the rutted track. 'No, there's just one more thing,' he said. 'I'm having a plough-man's in the Star if you care to join me.'

Hannah glanced at the man's rigid profile, not certain she had heard right. Was this Ross Hunter's way of apologising? But maybe he was right. She'd be letting down the nice woman from the train if she just disappeared back to Glasgow without a word. And it had been eighteen hours since she last ate anything.

'Well . . . what did you think?' Maggie asked when Ross dropped Hannah off at the Corrieglen post office several hours later.

Hannah had the impression that the village postmistress had been waiting all afternoon to ask that. She lifted her shoulders in a shrug. 'What can I say? It's a lovely place.'

'Aye, it's bonnie right enough.' Maggie frowned. 'I'm sensing a 'but' coming.'

Hannah laughed. 'Actually, I loved the place, but I do have to discuss it with my children. It won't be enough that I like it.'

A few hours ago she was all for high-tailing it out of here, but that was before spending some more profitable time in the Corrieglen estate manager's company. The man hadn't exactly apologised, but she sensed he'd regretted the impression he'd given that he hadn't thought her capable of running the croft. He wouldn't have given her a conducted tour of Glenburn and pointed out the primary school, if he hadn't wanted her to accept the tenancy. He'd obviously altered his opinion of her — and she couldn't help wondering why.

Maggie was nodding. 'I'm guessing your bairns are very young?'

Hannah listed the children's ages, and as Maggie busied herself locking up the post office section for the night and tidying round the shop, she recalled how all four of them had searched the internet for an image of Lanrig, and described Robbie's excitement when he discovered it was right beside the river.

'The water flows fast down there. It can be a dangerous place for bairns,' Maggie warned.

Hannah assured her the boys were both strong swimmers, and little Holly was a determined student. But they would be careful.

The sun was setting as they closed the shop and walked next door to Maggie and Jake's cottage. As far as Hannah could see, the little village store was the only shop around, and Corrieglen had no pub. But to Hannah's mind it all added to the attraction of the place.

Mondays were quiet days for Corrieglen's post office, which was why Maggie had special permission to close it until lunchtime, which gave her a chance to spend the occasional weekend at her sister Mary's house in Inverness. With Jake keeping an eye on the shop when she got back, she'd been able to nip next door and make a cottage pie for their guest's evening meal.

Hannah didn't tell her about the

ploughman's she and Ross had eaten at the Star Inn, in Glenburn. Her hostess had gone to the trouble of preparing this tasty supper, so the least Hannah could do was to try some. But to her surprise, the bracing Highland air had given her an appetite.

'That was truly delicious, Maggie,' she said, mopping up the last of the gravy with a slice of the crusty bread Maggie had bought before leaving Inverness.

Jake got up and patted his wife's head, planting a kiss amongst the silver curls. 'She's the best cook this side of Inverness,' he said in his melodious Highland accent.

Maggie flapped a hand, shooing him away. 'Be off with you man, before you embarrass the both of us in front of our guest.'

'I'm with Jake,' Hannah laughed. 'That was definitely the best cottage pie I've ever tasted.' She patted her stomach, grinning when she caught Jake's wink as he left the room.

'What do you think you're doing?' Maggie asked as Hannah rose to help clear the table. 'You are a paying guest; you're not expected to do any work.'

Hannah ignored her, collecting and scraping the plates. 'What you were saying earlier, Maggie? You're right, of course. There's a big 'but' to be considered. For a start, I don't know the first thing about working a croft.' She glanced up. 'I boasted to Ross Hunter earlier that I was capable enough, but the fact is . . . I'm just not sure.'

'So Ross was questioning your abilities? Och, but you mustn't pay any attention to him. He's not the female sex's biggest fan.' She sighed. 'I might as well tell you, since you'll find out anyway if you decide to stick around. Ross had a difficult marriage. His wife, Laura, was a pleasant enough young woman. She just hated Corrieglen.'

Hannah stared at her. She couldn't imagine anyone hating this place. 'I take it she left him?'

Maggie nodded. 'Lock, stock and

barrel . . . And she took their boy with her. They're divorced now, of course, but Ross still doesn't get to see young Josh. He'll be almost eleven now.'

'I'd no idea,' Hannah said quietly. 'Poor man.'

'Now don't you go getting sorry for him. Ross Hunter is his own worst enemy. He's bitter, and he doesn't like new-comers.' She took the plate Hannah passed to her and slotted it into the dishwasher. 'Ross and the old laird . . . they're two of a kind. That's probably why they get along so well. Sir John won't make a move without Ross's approval.'

Hannah looked up from clearing away the tea things. 'Does that mean he'll have a say about who gets the tenancy of Lanrig?'

'Probably, but that won't affect you, Hannah. You'll have first refusal, having been married to Lizzie's nephew.'

'First refusal? Is someone else inter-ested?'

'Aye, Jess Guthrie's lad, Gil. He's a bad lot if ever I saw one.' She looked up, and Hannah saw the warning glint in her eyes. 'You don't want to get mixed up with that family. Jess is a tough one, and she could be vicious if you were to get on the wrong side of her.'

'Hmm . . . ' Hannah brushed the crumbs from Maggie's red gingham tablecloth into her cupped hand and shook them into the bin. 'Sounds like I'd have a ready-made enemy if I took the place on.'

'Och, never mind Jess. It's young Gil you would have to watch. He fancies himself as a bit of a ladies' man.'

Hannah smiled. 'I don't get too much attention from ladies' men these days, so I doubt if this Gil would be much of a problem.'

Maggie pressed her lips together and said nothing.

The last thing Hannah had been expecting as she sat down to breakfast next morning was for Ross to turn up. Yet there he was, large as life, climbing out of the Land Rover.

Maggie glanced to the window and tutted. 'Now what could he be wanting at this time of day?' She turned to put the frying pan back on the stove and was wiping her hands on her apron when Jake brought Ross into the kitchen. 'Ross . . . to what do we owe this pleasure?'

The newcomer gave a solemn nod before his eyes settled on Hannah. 'The laird would like to meet you before you leave, Mrs Maxwell.'

Hannah's brow knitted. 'But I don't know if I'll be taking the tenancy yet. I . . . I have to discuss it with my family.'

Ross shook his head. 'That's fine. Sir John realises that. I think he'd just like to meet you.'

Hannah's eyes went to the clock. 'I'm not sure . . . there's the train . . . '

'You won't miss your train. The laird just wants to make your acquaintance.'

Hannah bit her lip, glancing at Maggie, who was nodding enthusiastically. 'We'll if you're sure I won't miss my train . . . '

'You have my word.'

As Ross slung Hannah's bag into the back of his vehicle, Maggie rushed forward to give her a hug. 'Come back soon, Hannah — and bring those bairns of yours next time.'

Hannah gave Maggie's hand a squeeze. 'Thanks for everything.' She looked across to Jake's broad shape filling the doorway. 'You, too, Jake.'

The old man's face cracked into a smile. 'Aye, see you again, lassie.'

'Looks like you've made some friends there,' Ross said as they pulled out of the cottage's back yard.

Hannah looked back, smiling, and waved. 'Just what I was thinking,' she said.

Overnight rain had muddied the ground, and puddles lined the drive to the big estate house. Close to, it didn't look as imposing as Hannah had thought when she'd glimpsed it across the fields the previous day. It was more like a big farmhouse than the grand residence of the Laird of Corrieglen.

A black Labrador dog appeared from the open front door and sauntered towards them. But it was the woman who took Hannah's attention. She was reminded of a scene in Daphne Du Maurier's novel, *Rebecca*, when the heroine met the fearsome Mrs Danvers for the first time. The thought made her want to giggle. But the woman — short, sturdy, her greyish-black hair knotted in a tight bun at the back of her head — was watching their approach with narrowed eyes.

'This is Jess Guthrie,' Ross said curtly. 'Sir John's cook.'

'Housekeeper,' the woman corrected, turning hostile black eyes back on Hannah.

Ross was showing no attempt to explain Hannah's presence, so she stuck out her hand. 'I'm Hannah Maxwell.'

The woman took her hand in a limp grip and gave a nod. 'That's what I assumed.'

'Is Sir John in his office?' Ross didn't wait for an answer. He steered Hannah across the vast reception hall, where heads of long-dead stags eyed them from above with regal disdain. 'Ignore Jess. She's just being nosy.' He tapped his leg and the black dog lumbered after them.

The door to the laird's office was ajar and Ross knocked before entering. The room was small and lined with bookshelves crammed with old leather-bound volumes. The September morning was not cold, but chunky logs glowed red in the small fireplace.

The Laird of Corrieglen was sitting behind a desk littered with papers. He looked up as they came in, his eyes narrowing at the sight of Hannah. He didn't look as if he had a clue who she was. She glanced up suspiciously at Ross.

'This is Mrs Maxwell, Laird. Lizzie's relative. She's come to see Lanrig.'

The old man's eyes lit up. 'Of course,' he said, standing to greet his visitor. 'So you're coming to join us at Corrieglen?'

'Er . . . no.' Hannah shot Ross a look. 'I thought Mr Hunter had explained. I have to talk it all over with my family. It's a big step uprooting my children from their school.'

'We have a perfectly good school in the next village, Mrs Maxwell. Ewan Stewart, the head teacher, knows what he's doing, and I have no doubt that he will make sure your young 'uns settle in just fine.'

Hannah raised an eyebrow at Ross, but the laird hadn't finished. 'Has Ross explained the financial side of things? There's a nominal rent, nothing you won't be able to afford. And you can always sell your produce.' His blue eyes crinkled as he tried to remember. 'Lizzie used to sell her potatoes and eggs at that farmers' market in Glenburn.' Ross nodded. 'And if I remember right, she leased off the grazing rights for her pasture to one of the other crofters.' The laird gave an affected little cough. 'We turned a blind eye to that, as I remember.'

Hannah bit her lip, her eye on the clock. 'You're going to think me very rude, Sir John.' She threw a desperate look at Ross.

'I think Mrs Maxwell is getting anxious about catching her train. She's travelling back to Glasgow today.'

The laird stood up and the black Labrador, who had settled himself in front of the fire, sensing Ross was about to leave, also began scrambling to his feet, but his legs wobbled and he sat down heavily again.

Hannah bent to stroke him. 'Is the dog ill?'

Sir John cleared his throat, fumbling in his pocket for his pipe. It was a distraction, for Hannah hadn't missed the glint of tears in his eyes. 'The old chap's on his way out,' he said brusquely.

She held the dog's face and stroked his silky head as the sad blue eyes gazed back at her. 'How old is he?'

The laird raised an eyebrow at Ross.

'Moby's eleven,' Ross said. 'He's got

66

an infection, and he's allergic to antibiotics.'

'But there must be something you can do?'

He shrugged, stooping to pat Moby's head. 'Hopefully he might work his way through it, but he's not getting any younger.' He glanced at his watch. 'We'll have to hurry if you're going to catch that train.'

The laird held out his hand, and Hannah took it. 'Good of you to call in.' He smiled, turning to Ross. 'Well, man, don't keep this young lady chatting. She has a train to catch.'

Hannah held her tongue until they were back in the Land Rover. 'Was it my imagination, or did the laird seem a bit confused?'

For a second she thought Ross was going to smile, but it was more like a grimace. He sighed. 'Don't let the old boy fool you. He's just sad about Moby, but he can be sharp as a needle when it suits him. I think he imagines the role of the bungling old laird is what is expected of him.' He glanced down at her. 'He liked you.'

Hannah gave a wistful smile, glancing back at Corrieglen House. The dumpy figure of Jess Guthrie was at the window, and the woman wasn't waving farewell. Even from this distance Hannah could see her scowl.

The train was in the station when they arrived and they had to sprint to catch it. Puffing, Hannah hopped on board and rolled down the window, leaning out to wave.

Ross stared after her, and his brow furrowed. Hannah Maxwell wouldn't be back . . . not now that she knew what a bunch of oddballs they were at Corrieglen.

4

One look at her daughter's face told
Peggy what she'd been dreading — that
the visit to the Highlands had been a
good one. The glitter of excitement in
her eyes was unmistakable. If she'd
been a better mother she'd have been
happy for Hannah and the children.
They so deserved this unexpected slice
of good luck. She just couldn't bear to
lose them.

'How was it?' she asked stiffly.

Hannah pushed back her hair and sat
down. 'Let's get the children through
and I'll tell you all together.'

Holly was first to appear, hearing her
mother's voice; she rushed into kitchen,
reaching up to throw her plump arms
around her mother's neck.

'Hey,' Hannah laughed, stooping to
hug her back. 'Did you miss me?'

Robbie and Jamie crowded in, firing

one excited question after another at her. Hannah put up a hand in a hopeless bid to calm the three of them down. 'Have you all been good for Granny and Gramps?'

A chorus of assurances rang round the room. Hannah raised an eyebrow at her mother. Peggy nodded, smiling.

'They've been watching the clock all morning waiting for you,' Hannah's dad joined them. She didn't miss the look that passed between her parents and felt a tiny stab of disquiet. If she decided to move it would affect their lives as much as hers. Could she really deprive them of their grandchildren?

Peggy watched them with a wan smile. She had to ask, even if she already knew the answer. 'I take it everything went well up there?'

Hannah's eyes shone, and she nodded. 'It's a lovely place, Mum.' She patted Holly's curls, organising the three children into the places her mother had set for tea. As they tucked into their fish fingers, chips, and crunchy salad, Alec drew his daughter aside.

'Did you see this wee place, then?'

Hannah glanced back at the children and, satisfied that they were all still happily munching, nodded towards the front room. She hadn't wanted to discuss her trip this soon. She still wasn't certain what her decision would be . . . or was she?

Peggy had followed them through. 'Well?' she said, sinking into one of the two upholstered fireside chairs.

Keeping half an ear on the chatter from next door, Hannah took a breath and began to describe the croft house and the surrounding land, enthusing about the friendly welcome she had been given by Maggie and Jake. 'I even met the laird,' she said, trying to keep the excitement out of her voice.

Peggy squared her shoulders. 'I see.' Her voice was icy.

Alec Gilmore gave a little cough. 'Have you thought about how you would live up there, Hannah? From what you've said, this Lanrig place is miles from anywhere. I can't imagine there would be many jobs close by. It's not as though you could just jump on a bus in remote places like that.'

'It's not that remote, Dad. Lanrig is only a mile or so from Corrieglen, but you're right, I would have to find some kind of work. Aunt Lizzie's money won't support us for long.'

'Sounds like you've already decided to move up there,' Peggy said, turning away to hide the sparkle of tears in her eyes.

Hannah jumped up to give her mother a hug, holding onto her hand as she turned to her father. 'Now, listen you two . . . if we do decide to move . . . then it will be a joint decision. I want everyone to be happy about it.' But from the look on her parents' faces, that wasn't going to happen. So much still had to be considered. The biggest wrench would be for her mum and dad, especially her mother. Peggy spent so much time with the children, keeping an eye on them when Hannah was working, collecting them from school, often making their supper. She'd be devastated if they all moved so far away.

Hannah moistened her lips. 'I need your support on this. I can't afford to get it wrong. The last thing I want is for the four of us to move up to the croft, and then discover a few months down the line that it was a mistake.' She glanced from one to the other. 'So what I suggest is that we all meet up at my house, get round the kitchen table, and discuss the pros and cons.' She squeezed her mother's hand. 'What do you say?'

Her parents exchanged looks, and then Peggy nodded. She still wasn't happy, but she gave Hannah a reluctant grin. 'When do you want us to come?'

The ten-minute drive home in her dad's little Mini was noisy, with the three excited children in the back, all firing questions at her. But she didn't mind. She was happy with how she had handled things. Until she had actually said the words, she hadn't considered holding a family conference. Now she was certain it was a good idea.

Peggy and Alec came round the following evening, but they knew further discussion was unnecessary. They had already decided they must support the move. Once the decision had been made, the whole family got involved with preparations. Hannah's dad helped her find an affordable and reliable second-hand car. The nine-year-old green Hyundai estate she'd settled on might not have been the trendiest of vehicles, but it seemed the most practical for their new life.

She settled her business with the building society, handed in her notice at work, hired a removal firm, and informed the head teacher at the children's school that the family was moving.

It was still dark on the morning they set off for the Highlands. The previous evening had been emotional. Even though they would be living only a few hours' drive away, she could see her parents were upset. Her mum was putting on a brave face, but she wasn't fooling Hannah. Hannah put her arms around her. 'You and Dad will be up to visit us in few weeks' time, and I'll be on the phone every day. So you see, there is nothing to worry about.' She turned to her father. 'Tell her, Dad.'

To Hannah's dismay, she saw that there were tears in his eyes too. It was all she could do to dissuade them from getting up at four a.m. the next morning to wave them off. She'd been dreading this final wrench, but when the time came to walk out of her house for the last time, she felt remarkably calm.

Her marriage to Brian had been over in all but name long before he died. The years had changed him. He'd become secretive, a loner . . . a liar who'd gambled himself into debt and ultimately cost his family their home. Hannah had seen no way out when the eviction notice had arrived — and then this miracle had happened! Now a new home beckoned, and a whole new life was opening up for them. She had nothing to feel nostalgic about.

With everyone settled in the car she glanced back, and for a split second, felt a jolt of panic. Could she be sure she was doing the right thing? But it was too late to back out now. The little terraced house wasn't their home any more.

She turned the key in the ignition, and they set off into the dark morning.

5

It was late afternoon when they drove into Corrieglen. The estate had arranged to leave the keys to Lanrig at the post office and Hannah was looking forward to seeing Maggie and Jake again. She didn't have long to wait. Maggie had been watching for them and came running out to the car as they pulled up.

Holly, who had slept for the last hour of the trip, was suddenly awake. She rubbed her eyes, looking around. 'Are we here, Mummy? Is this our new house?'

'Not quite, sweetheart,' Hannah smiled, glancing at Jamie who, from the look of him, had also just woken up.

Only Robbie was wide awake, glancing about him with an expression of displeasure. 'Is this it?' His lip curled in distaste. He looked like he'd just been asked to eat a plate of worms.

Before Hannah had a chance to

respond, Maggie was opening the car door and ushering them all inside. 'You poor wee things. You'll be wanting a hot drink and something to eat after your long journey.'

Hannah gave a grateful sigh. 'You're an angel, Maggie. A drink would be so welcome, but we won't stay for long. I want to get up to the croft while there's still enough light for the children to see it.'

Maggie swept concerned eyes over the three children. 'Are you sure you wouldn't rather just leave that till the morning? These wee mites look done in.'

Hannah looked at the children and smiled. 'You're right, they do all look a bit shattered. We can drive up to the croft in the morning.'

Holly's face crumpled into a yell. 'Want to see croftie place now!' She stamped her feet.

Jamie joined her protest. 'Aw, Mum . . . Let's go now.'

Hannah glanced at Robbie, who

raised his shoulders in a disinterested shrug. But there was a spark in his eyes that told her he was just as keen as the others to see Lanrig.

'OK,' Hannah relented. 'We can drive up there now for a quick look round.' She turned. 'Can you give us an hour, Maggie?'

The postmistress frowned. 'If that's what you want. There will be a meal on the table for you when you get back, and I'll have your rooms ready.'

She watched as they drove out of the village and felt a little jolt of nostalgia. She'd been fond of old Lizzie Sutherland, but life moved on. It would be good for the old croft to have some new blood about the place. As she went back inside, she had a feeling that nothing would ever be quite the same in Corrieglen.

The late autumn sun was beginning to sink low in the hills behind Lanrig as the family arrived, bumping along the same rutted road Hannah had travelled with Ross Hunter. She had been nursing a vague hope that he might have turned up to welcome them. But why should he? She got the distinct impression last time that he wasn't exactly happy about her taking on the croft. Well, whether Ross Hunter liked it or not, they were here now — and they were going nowhere!

Holly and Jamie bounced out of the car as Hannah brought it to a stop in the yard. 'It's a gingerbread house!' Holly squealed, and did a funny little jig around the yard.

Jamie's eyes were on the river he could see glinting at the bottom of the field. 'Cool.' He grinned.

Hannah glanced round at Robbie. His expression wasn't quite as disinterested as before. She'd take this as a positive sign. It was a huge upheaval in their young lives. She was doing it for all the right reasons, but she could understand the children's reluctance to move away from their friends and the security of their old life — except that it hadn't been secure at all. She sighed.

She really hadn't had much choice. They were lucky to have this place.

Hannah unlocked the back door and they all followed her into the kitchen. She flicked a switch and the room was flooded with harsh, cold light. It had looked different the last time, with sunlight slanting through the windows and a view of the river sparkling beyond the pasture. Now in the harsh electric light she saw it through the children's eyes, and she shivered. 'It will all look different once we get our own furniture in,' she said brightly, trying to hide her dismay at the three solemn little faces.

The children trailed around after her as she went from room to room, trying to inject enthusiasm into her voice as she told them where all their furniture would go. They had all grown very quiet. She gathered them all into her arms.

'You know what? I think it's time we all went back to Mrs Morrison's for tea. I know for a fact that she's prepared something very special for us.'

'Will it be fish fingers and chips?' Holly's eyes lit up.

'I think it's going to be a surprise,' Hannah said, crossing her fingers. She doubted very much if Maggie had ever dished up fish fingers in her life.

It was almost dark when they got back to the village, and the post office was closed and locked. Hannah parked the car and took the children around to the side door of the cottage. Delicious cooking smells wafted from the kitchen as Maggie hustled them all through to the comfy front room, where a cheery log fire was crackling in the grate.

'You know where the bathroom is, Hannah, if the children want to wash before tea.' She glanced around at the tired faces. 'It's steak pie. I hope you like that.'

'Yum,' Holly said, licking her lips, the fish fingers now a distant memory.

Maggie and Jake had pushed together a couple of the tables they used for their B&B guests. The children took their seats and lost no time tucking into their generous portions of pie.

Hannah went to the kitchen and put an arm round Maggie's shoulder. 'Thanks for doing this, Maggie. It's just what they needed.'

Maggie glanced up as she dished up three more portions for the adults. 'How did it go up at Lanrig?' She narrowed her eyes. 'Did the children like the place?'

Hannah grimaced. 'They weren't exactly thrilled.' She remembered the three serious little faces. They'd all hated the old croft, she could tell. But it was too late to turn back now, even if she'd wanted to. They were staying. The children would grow to love the place; it just might take a little longer than she'd hoped.

Maggie handed her a plateful of food. 'Give it time, Hannah. Lanrig is the kind of place that grows on you . . . you'll see.'

Dawn was still seeping into the eastern sky when Hannah got up next morning and had a quick shower before following the smell of coffee down to the kitchen. 'I can't believe they're all still asleep,' she told Maggie.

'It's the Highland air.' Maggie grinned, turning the sausages that were sizzling in the pan. 'It's pretty powerful if you're not used to it.' She glanced at the clock. 'What time did the removal people give?'

'Anywhere from eight onwards.' She felt a flutter of excitement.

'Well that gives you all time to get something inside yourselves,' Maggie said, glancing up from her frying pan. 'It could be a long day for all of you.'

Hannah put a hand on her stomach. 'I couldn't eat a thing right now, but I'm sure the children won't refuse.'

The smell of sizzling sausages and bacon had reached Robbie. Cooked breakfasts were a special weekend treat at home, but they weren't at home. He climbed out of bed, trying not to wake Jamie and Holly, who were in bunk beds by the window. They must have heard him moving about, for they both stirred, struggling to sit up.

Holly rubbed her eyes sleepily, her face crumpling into a wail as she stared around the unfamiliar room. 'Mummy!!' she yelled, her eyes filling with panic.

Jamie frowned. 'Shut up that racket, Holly.' He could smell the sausages and his tummy was rumbling in anticipation.

The door opened and Hannah came in. Holly shot out of bed, her bottom lip still trembling.

'Hey ... what's all this about?' Hannah stroked Holly's tousled curls. 'I happen to know there's a yummy breakfast waiting for all of you downstairs.' She held Holly at arm's length and tilted her head. 'How do sausages, bacon and baked beans sound?'

Fifteen minutes later, Robbie, Jamie and Holly were washed, dressed, and sitting at the table in Maggie's dining room, enormous helpings of food in front of them.

'That's the way.' Maggie grinned, putting another rack of hot toast on the table. 'Tuck in. I like to see bairns appreciating their food.'

They were certainly doing that, Hannah thought. But any idea she'd had of nipping up to the croft to organise the removal men while the three of them ate their breakfast slowly slipped away as she watched them. Holly's expression was still sulky, even though her cheeks bulged with the mouthful of toast she was munching. Slipping out now might cause a riot. She sighed. No. They would all drive up to Lanrig together, and she would have to do her best to keep her brood from under the feet of the removal team.

Even Robbie's face brightened when he saw the huge van parked at the back of the croft. 'Is all our stuff in there? . . . Our computer?'

Hannah nodded. She'd checked with Ross that broadband access would be available at the croft.

They couldn't have wished for a better day. The sun shone from a blue sky and the little cottage looked as pretty as when she'd first set eyes on it.

Two burly men were leaning against the front of the removal van and a third was by the low stone wall, gazing down to the river. Hannah saw Robbie's eyes stray to it, and thought she caught a spark of excitement there. The removal team looked up as she and the children approached.

'Nice spot you have here,' one of them commented, nodding towards the river, which was sparkling in the early morning sunshine. 'Holiday home, is it?'

No,' Hannah muttered, striding past them to unlock the back door of the croft. 'It certainly isn't a holiday home.' She ignored their look of surprise.

The move proceeded like clockwork. Hannah was grateful she had been organised enough to label each box and piece of furniture, allocating it to its new place in the cottage. The first time she'd seen the place she had thought it small in comparison to their Glasgow house; but now, as the rooms filled, she realised that it was actually much bigger. The kitchen and sitting room took up the full ground floor area. They were huge, especially the kitchen. She was imagining mealtimes around their big wooden table.

The children's voices drifted in from the front pasture, where they were playing. She'd put Robbie in charge of looking after the two younger ones and he appeared to be enjoying his new responsibility. He'd unearthed a football and, judging by the squeals and laughter, they seemed to be having fun.

Ross Hunter stopped the Land Rover at the top of the lane and surveyed the removal operations. He thought of offering his help, but from what he could see, Hannah Maxwell already had more than enough muscle at her disposal.

The three children he could see chasing a ball around the field were older than he'd expected. Somehow he'd imagined her family to be young . . . babies, even. Why had he thought that? He frowned. Hannah was nowhere to be seen. He pursed his lips, wondering if he should leave them all to it, then sighed and moved the vehicle into first gear before bumping along the lane to park in front of the removal van.

Hannah saw him coming and felt her heart quicken. She'd wondered if Ross would turn up, and now here he was. Wiping her hands on her apron, she went to meet him.

'Mr Hunter.' She put out her hand, meeting his steely gaze, searching for a glint of welcome.

He glanced at the activities going on around him, narrowing his eyes. 'The laird thought you might need some help.'

The laird, not you, Hannah thought. He was here because his employer had told him to be. Her first instinct was to send him packing. If he couldn't offer his help out of simple neighbourliness, then she didn't need it. She sighed. She knew that wasn't true. She needed a strong pair of arms to help her assemble the beds and move the furniture into the desired places. The removal people had been accommodating, but assembling furniture wasn't part of their job and, judging by how often she caught them checking their watches, they were obviously working to a timetable.

She put a smile on her face. 'That was very thoughtful of the laird.' Just for a second, she thought she caught a look in his eyes. Had it been embarrassment?

Now that most of the furniture had been brought indoors, the place was beginning to look cosy. She'd left Ross upstairs assembling the children's beds, and the removal team seemed to be getting ready to leave. Hannah found her purse and pulled out a £20 note, offering it to the man who appeared to be in charge, but to her surprise he shook his head, smiling. He nodded in the direction of the upstairs bedrooms.

'Your man's already seen us all right.'

Hannah swallowed. Ross Hunter was hardly 'her man', but there was no point in explaining that to these people.

From the looks on their faces she could tell their tip had been substantial. She followed them to the door, calling her thanks. She waved when she saw Maggie's car pulling up.

'Just a pot of soup and some sandwiches,' Maggie said, heaving the car boot open, grabbing a big plastic box and handing it to Hannah. She reached in for the heavy soup pot and nodded to the Land Rover. 'I see Ross is here.'

'He's upstairs assembling the children's beds.' There was no way she was going to ask him to put up her own big pine bed, even though she had no idea how she would manage to do it on her own.

'Well good for him,' Maggie said.

'The laird told him to come,' Hannah said.

Maggie's quick glance told her she was being unfair. Ross didn't have to do all the work he had put in on her behalf this morning. He could have just helped the others shift a few pieces of furniture and left it at that. Judging by the banging and hammering noises coming from upstairs, he was making a good job of what he was doing.

The dishes were still packed in a huge cardboard box on the kitchen floor, and Maggie helped Hannah to hunt through the packaging for the bowls and mugs they needed. Seeing Maggie's arrival, the children had come running in and were now enjoying the apparently hilarious task of 'helping' the rummage.

Hannah, on her knees by the packing case, and laughing at her inability to keep the children in order, hadn't heard Ross's approach. She looked up as he came in, pushing back a dark strand of hair that had fallen over her flushed face.

He hesitated for a second, and then cocked an eyebrow. 'Can I help?'

'Oh.' Hannah struggled to her feet. 'Mr Hunter.'

Out of the corner of her eye she caught Maggie's surprised frown and knew she was wondering why she was being so formal. It wasn't a question she could answer, except to say that she felt more comfortable keeping this man at arm's length.

Ross nodded a greeting to Maggie, and his eyes travelled over the faces of the three giggling children.

'Robbie, Jamie and Holly,' Hannah said. Then turning to the children, she added, 'This is Mr Hunter. He's . . . emm . . . he's been helping us.'

They all glanced up at Ross and he inclined his head. To Hannah's surprise his mouth curved into a smile, and before she realised what she was saying she had invited him to stay and share their lunch. 'Maggie seems to have brought enough food to feed an army,' she said.

Maggie struggled up and put her hands on her hips. 'Yes, why don't you stay, Ross? There's plenty here.'

But Ross shook his head. 'No, it's kind of you, but I must be getting on.' Before they had a chance to reply, he'd turned and was striding out the door.

It wasn't until Maggie had gone and they had unpacked the rest of the crockery that Hannah and the children explored upstairs. Ross hadn't only assembled the boys' bunk beds and Holly's little one, but he'd also placed them neatly against the walls. The rooms already looked cosy.

'Can we get our toys out now, Mummy?' Holly was using her most persuasive voice.

'Yes, Mum, can we?' Jamie pleaded.

Hannah smiled and ruffled Holly's hair. 'I think that's a good idea.' She could hear their whoops of delight as she went out and along the landing to her own room.

She reached the door and then stopped. Her mouth fell open. The huge, heavy pine bed had not only been fully assembled and pushed into place, but her bedside tables had been positioned on either side. Her hand went to her mouth. Maybe she had misjudged Ross Hunter after all.

The day had been such a busy one that there had been no time for Hannah to dwell on feelings. But now, with the children all asleep upstairs, she experienced a sudden surge of loneliness. She got up and began wandering about the cottage. It was all so quiet. Was this what it was going to be like from now on? Over the past few days she'd been feeling like a new woman, but now all the old insecurities came flooding back. There was no lovely Laura next door to invite in for a chat. And her mother was hundreds of miles away.

Somewhere out in the night an owl hooted. Hannah slipped on her coat and opened the front door. The moon was casting a silvery light over the pasture, playing on the ripples on the river, making the water glisten like moonbeams. She listened and heard the hooting again. It was coming from the direction of the old elm trees at the top of the lane. Down by the river, something splashed. Could it be an otter? She would ask Ross if there were any otters around here. Maybe there were badgers and foxes out there, too. The children would love that.

Hannah took a deep breath and hugged herself. Maybe she wasn't so alone after all. She turned and went back inside, closing the door quietly behind her as she went to the stairs and climbed up to bed.

'Mummy, Mummy, there's a pony in our field.'

Hannah shook herself awake. Jamie and Holly were bouncing on her bed. She struggled to sit up. 'A pony?'

'Come and see, Mummy.' Holly tugged at Hannah's arm. 'I think he's hungry.'

Hannah frowned, throwing back the duvet as she reached for her dressing gown. Jamie and Holly bounded down the stairs ahead of her. The front door had been flung wide and she could see Robbie circling a large grey animal. It was a pony — an enormous great pony! 'Come back here this minute, Robbie!' she yelled.

'It's fine, Mum. He likes me, see?' He threw his arms around the pony's neck and the animal struggled, trying to free itself.

Hannah had visions of it suddenly rearing up and trampling her son. Trying to keep the panic out of her voice, she called to Robbie again. 'I said come here.'

Holly was bouncing excitedly by her side. 'I want to ride him. Can I ride him?'

Robbie was doing a good job of pretending not to hear her. The gate into the pasture was further along the track. Her son could be under the animal's hooves by the time she got down there. She hitched up her dressing gown and clambered over the low wall, the whoops of delight from Jamie and Holly ringing in her ears. She approached with caution, holding out a restraining hand.

'Move slowly behind me, Robbie,' she instructed.

Robbie stared at her, grinning. 'He

won't bite, Mum. Look.' He ruffled the animal's straggly grey mane. 'He likes me.'

A vehicle's door slammed at the back of the croft, and they all looked up as Ross appeared from the side of the building. He stopped in his tracks at the sight of the pony. 'Ah . . . You've met Erin, then.'

'Erin?' Hannah repeated slowly, still eyeing the animal with caution.

Ross nodded. 'I thought she might have wandered back here.' He vaulted the wall in one easy movement. She was glad he hadn't witnessed her own ungainly clamber over it moments earlier. It was bad enough that he'd found her standing in the middle of this pasture in her dressing gown, even if she had been there to protect her son.

Ross strode towards them, holding a hand out to the pony. He was clutching a carrot. 'Poor old girl. You're missing your friend, aren't you?' He held out the carrot and patted the pony's head. The animal turned her huge mournful eyes on him and bared her teeth to take the offering in one gentle movement. Ross turned to Hannah.

'Erin was Lizzie's pony.' He raised his eyes and nodded across the fields. 'Your neighbour, old Sandy Crawford . . . he has a croft over at Moraig, and has been looking after her. She must have got out of her barn and wandered back across the fields.' He gave the pony an affectionate grin. 'You just wanted to come home old girl, didn't you?'

'You see, Mum,' Robbie chimed in, 'she belongs here. She's *our* pony now.'

Ross raised an eyebrow at Hannah and she threw up her hands. 'I know nothing about ponies. How could I possibly look after her? Besides,' she lowered her voice, squinting out to the distant hills, 'it'll be enough of a struggle to feed ourselves, let alone . . . ' She flapped her hand at the pony, which was now looking at her with the same trusting stare she had given Ross. 'Let alone Erin, here.'

'Oh, you don't have to worry about

feeding her. I'll bring all the food she can eat.' He sighed. 'I'd take her myself, but I just don't have the space back at the lodge. Anyway, she's used to this place. She just needs people to love her again.' His glance travelled to the three eager faces. 'And by the look of things she's already found them.'

Robbie fixed her with a grin. 'Can we, Mum? Can we keep her?'

It was the most animated Hannah had seen the boy since the move to Lanrig. She threw up her hands and rolled her eyes heavenwards. 'Do I have a choice?'

Robbie punched the air. 'Yes!' he hollered.

The animal was nuzzling Ross's arm and he lovingly stroked her head. 'Lizzie rescued her, you know. She's come all the way from Eriskay, in the Outer Hebrides. She's a very rare breed now. You're actually rather privileged to have her here.'

Hannah frowned. 'How do you mean, rescued?'

'Erin is a working pony. She belonged to a friend of Lizzie and Seth's, an old crofter in Eriskay. When he died a couple of years back, Lizzie offered to take Erin. She paid for the pony's passage on the ferry to the mainland — and it wasn't cheap.' He pressed his lips together in a hard line. 'That's the kind of woman she was.'

Hannah looked up and saw the sadness in his eyes and realised with surprise that he'd been really fond of the old lady. 'I wish I could have met her,' she said quietly.

His eyes narrowed as he looked down at her. She squared her shoulders and glanced away. She knew he was thinking she would never live up to the old lady's legend.

Hannah yanked the tie of her dressing gown tighter, and wondered how she was going to get back over the wall with any dignity. But she needn't have worried, because Ross had already turned and was striding back to his Land Rover.

Jamie and Holly had launched into their excited bounce again. 'Is Erin really ours, now?' Jamie's eyes were wide with excitement.

Hannah pursed her lips and looked back to the pony. 'So it would seem,' she sighed.

Before she had reached the cottage door, Ross had reappeared, carrying a bale of hay, his lively black and white Collie bouncing around his feet. He held up the bale. 'I'll put some of this in Erin's trough and leave the rest in the shed.'

Hannah couldn't think of anything to say, so she nodded. 'I have to get the children dressed and give them their breakfast.' It was still very early and she wondered if Ross had eaten yet. 'You . . . umm . . . you're welcome to join us if you like,' she offered hesitantly.

He half turned. 'I've already had something, thanks,' he said curtly, leaving Hannah wishing she'd never offered. It was the second time in as many days that he'd refused her invitation. She wouldn't be asking a third time.

When he'd gone, and she'd supervised the early morning ablutions, Hannah glanced out at the pony as she set the table for the children's breakfasts. How hard could it be to look after a pony? Lizzie seemed to have managed it all right. And besides, the children already seemed to love the animal. If looking after an old pony meant putting herself out for the sake of her children, then there was no contest . . . and she *was* doing this for the children, wasn't she?

She remembered Ross Hunter's expression of affection towards Erin, and for a fleeting instant wondered how she would feel if he looked at her like that. There had been real compassion in the serious green eyes. It was a pity he couldn't extend that same consideration to people.

6

Glenburn Primary School was ominously quiet as Hannah and the children crossed the deserted playground a few days later. She'd rung earlier and been told to report to reception.

'I think it must be this way.' She tried to sound encouraging, but she hadn't missed the uneasy looks the three of them were exchanging.

Muted sounds came from the classrooms as they passed — the shuffling of feet, desk lids closing, and a teacher's voice murmuring as she walked along the rows of desks checking her pupils' work.

'Mrs Maxwell?' They all turned. The man striding towards them was tall, wiry, with thinning brown hair and a craggy smile. 'Ewan Stewart. I'm the head teacher here.' His hand shot out for Hannah to shake. 'Please come this way.' He waved in the direction of his office. Hannah turned, giving the children another encouraging smile, as she ushered them ahead of her.

'So, you've come to live in our little community,' Mr Stewart said over his shoulder as they followed him along the corridor. He didn't wait for a response. 'Well, you are all very welcome. We don't get too many new families moving into Corrieglen.'

They'd reached his door and he pushed it open, indicating for Hannah go in and sit. He glanced down at the papers on his desk. 'Mr Scott, the headmaster of the children's previous school, has sent me their progress reports. I see we're actually ahead of them in some subjects.' He looked up, smiling at the children. 'But I'm sure you will all catch up quickly. Now if there is anything you don't understand, or are worried about, just speak up. We're all here to help you.' He turned to Hannah. 'If I could just take a few details for the forms?'

She nodded, answering all the official questions as Mr Stewart scribbled them down in a hand she suspected that only he could decipher.

'Fine,' he said at last. 'I think that covers everything.' He took off his spectacles and leaned back in his chair, smiling at Robbie, Jamie and Holly. 'Would you like me to tell you something about our little school?' Hannah nodded and the others stared at him.

'We have sixty-two pupils.' He gave a little grin. 'Sixty-five when you three start on Monday. The children are split into three classes. Mrs Richardson takes the younger ones, Miss Cameron looks after the middle group, and I teach the older children. We also have three class helpers.' He ignored Hannah's raised eyebrow. 'Most of the children, like you, live a mile or two away and are brought to school and taken home each day by special school buses.' He glanced at Hannah. 'Don't worry; I'll arrange all that. The bus can pick the children up at the top of the lane at Lanrig at 8.30 a.m. on Mondays, and drop them back at the same point around 3.30 p.m. each afternoon.' He reached into his desk drawer and brought out a sheet of paper. 'This gives details of our school uniform. Not technically essential, but most of the children wear it.'

'And mine will be no exception, Mr Stewart,' Hannah said, a little more defensively than she had intended. She saw the head teacher's brow furrow slightly.

'Of course,' he said. 'I just meant whenever it is convenient.' His face creased into a kindly smile. 'It can be a stressful time moving into a new home, especially a remote place like Lanrig.'

'You know the croft?'

'Well, of course I do. A new family moving in up there is big news in these parts, Mrs Maxwell. You're our local celebrities at the moment.'

Hannah felt herself colouring. 'I expect you knew the previous tenant, Mrs Sutherland?'

Ewan Stewart nodded. 'We all knew Lizzie. She was a great friend of Glenburn Primary. She hosted many school visits to Lanrig.'

Hannah raised an eyebrow, wondering if the same would be expected of her.

Ewan was nodding, remembering. 'There was nothing that Lizzie liked better than showing the young ones over her fields and explaining the old crofting ways to them. She had endless patience. The children loved her.'

Hannah's own three were becoming decidedly restless. Mr Stewart got to his feet, signaling their business had concluded. He smiled and nodded to each of the three little faces. 'So we'll see you all on Monday, then!'

Holly gave him her most endearing smile. She was happy the meeting was over. Robbie and Jamie merely offered solemn nods. As they all filed out of the tiny office, Ewan touched Hannah's arm. 'Don't worry about them. I'm sure they will all settle in just fine. My own two children, Becky and Rory, will make sure they look after your brood.'

'Thank you.' Hannah smiled back. 'That's kind of you.' She took his extended hand again.

'Not at all. Settling into a new community is always stressful. And I really mean it . . . if there is anything we can do to help, then you must say.'

Everyone was being so kind to them. She felt a tear prick her eye. The last thing she wanted was to be thought of as the poor widow woman with three young ones to bring up on her own, but wasn't that exactly what she was? She blinked back the wetness, hoping Mr Stewart hadn't noticed, and murmured her thanks.

Monday came round faster than any of them had expected. Hannah had decided to drive the children to school herself. It tugged at her heart to watch the three of them go through the gates. She almost rushed into the playground to throw her arms around Holly when the forlorn little face turned back to gaze at her with huge, imploring eyes.

But this was something that her children had to do on their own. She told herself that they would soon make new friends . . . that moving to Corrieglen had been the right thing to do.

Only when she was alone did the uncertainties begin to creep back — the sadness of Brian's death, the burden of pending homelessness. They could have struggled on, staying with her parents until a council house was available, but it would still have meant upheaval, and there was no telling where they might have been sent. The children would still have had to change schools and live in a strange, unfamiliar environment. The bills would have continued to mount, stretching her meager income to cover even the most basic needs.

Here they had a roof over their heads, and the cushion of what remained of Lizzie's £15,000 bequest. She would just have to find a job.

Ewan Stewart came into the playground with a middle-aged woman whom Hannah presumed was Mrs Richardson. Both of them smiled in her direction as they organised their charges into lines. Holly turned for a final, beseeching look at Hannah. But Mrs Richardson was there, taking Holly's hand, chatting encouragingly to her as they followed the other children inside the school.

Hannah bit her lip, staring after them as they all trooped inside. It was some moments before she could tear herself away. She sat at the wheel of her car, telling herself it was ridiculous to feel so bereft. Would it be like this every morning after the children left for school? It was up to her now to be both mother and father to them. She sighed, starting the engine and turning the car back in the direction of home.

She spotted Ross Hunter's Land Rover in the yard as soon as she turned into the lane. He came striding out of the barn, brushing hay from his jeans, raising his arm in greeting when he saw her. Hannah pulled the Hyundai alongside his vehicle and got out.

'Good morning, Mr Hunter.'

Ross nodded, surveying her from under his lowered brows. Did the man never smile? He half turned back to the barn. 'I brought hay for Erin — not that she'll need it at the moment, when there is plenty of grazing. It's a standby for when the snow comes.'

'What? Oh, the pony . . . that was kind of you.'

He gave her a quizzical frown. 'I said I would.'

Hannah smiled. 'So you did.' She locked the car, then realised how unnecessary that was in such an isolated spot. She shrugged. 'Force of habit.'

Ross nodded. 'We don't get too many burglaries in this part of the world, but I suppose you had to be more careful in Glasgow.'

'You're lucky not having to worry about that kind of thing up here.'

Ross's brows knitted. 'I wouldn't say that. We have a different kind of crime.'

She waited for him to explain, but he showed no inclination to do so. 'Is there something I should know?'

He squinted out across the river to the forest of fir trees climbing up the other side. 'We have our fair share of poachers on the estate. I should keep on locking your property if I were you.'

'Right . . . well, thank you. I will.' She turned towards the house. 'I was just about to put to put the kettle on if you fancy a cup of tea.'

He hesitated for a split second before shaking his head. 'Thanks, but I should get on.' He was already striding back to the Land Rover. She'd been dismissed. She felt a little stab of anger at the man's behaviour. Ross Hunter was the only person she'd met here who showed absolutely no desire to be friendly towards her. He was different with Robbie, Jamie and Holly. They already liked him. It was just her he had a problem with.

'What about the hay?' she called after him. 'How much of it am I supposed to give the pony?'

He turned, arching an eyebrow.

'I told you. It's for the winter. Erin's

a tough little critter and she'll be happy enough with the grazing for the time being. I'll call by to check up on her.'

'Well, thanks for that,' she muttered under her breath, as his vehicle sprung into life, and he swung it back up the bumpy lane.

Hannah's worries about the children settling into their new school had now been superseded by concern over Ross's attitude. He obviously didn't like her. Well, too bad, because she wasn't going anywhere! She warmed her hands on the mug of hot tea and gazed out the kitchen window to the pony in the pasture. She looked content enough. It was Hannah who had the problem. She had to find a job!

A knock at the back door made her start and she got up, wondering if the surly estate manager had decided to take up her offer of a drink after all. But the caller wasn't Ross Hunter. The woman who stood there was as tall as herself, with kindly, dark eyes. Her long brown hair was caught back in a clip, but strands had escaped, giving her face a windswept look. Hannah could see the toes of brown leather boots peeping from the hem of a flowing floral skirt.

'I'm Bethany Stewart.' The caller smiled. 'Ewan's wife . . . your children started school today?'

'Oh, of course,' Hannah laughed. 'I'm sorry; my head seems to be all over the place today. You're the headmaster's wife?'

Bethany nodded. 'I hope this isn't an intrusion? I just stopped by to welcome you to the area . . . and to give you this.' She thrust a plastic box at Hannah. 'It's shortbread . . . my specialty.'

'Oh, how kind of you.' Hannah forced a smile. She wasn't really in the mood for company this morning, but she couldn't be rude to the woman. She glanced back to the kitchen. 'I'm just having some tea. There's plenty in the pot if you fancy a cup.'

Bethany came in and gave a gasp of delight, taking in the fresh gingham curtains, scrubbed wooden table, washing machine, microwave oven beside the red ceramic crock pot, and the gleaming stainless steel utensils hanging from a rack on the wall. Hannah had lit the Aga before the children got up and the kitchen was warm and cosy.

'You've got this place looking really homely already.' She clasped her hands. 'I do hope you will all be happy here. We're a very friendly little community, so if there's anything you need . . . anything at all . . . just let Ewan or myself know.'

Hannah smiled. 'Thank you, I appreciate that.'

Bethany glanced at the window and smiled out at the contented pony nibbling the grass. 'I see Erin's come back.'

Hannah grimaced. 'We seem to have inherited her.' She looked up and added hopefully, 'I don't suppose you know anything about looking after horses?'

'I would imagine Ross is your man for that.'

'We'll, yes, but he's not exactly forthcoming on the subject. He seems to think we should know all about keeping animals, which of course we don't.'

Bethany got up and came to stand beside her. 'You haven't done anything like this before, have you, Hannah?'

'It shows, does it?' She looked up and saw that Bethany's dark eyes had softened.

'And yet you still came here,' she said quietly.

Hannah sipped her tea, turning away so the other woman would not see her eyes misting over. The last thing she wanted was to be pitied in this new community. She'd had enough of that during her marriage. She took a breath. 'We needed to make a move, have a fresh start. My husband died a year ago you see, and . . . ' Her voice shook. 'Things have been tough for us.'

She'd no idea how much Bethany knew of her past, but there seemed to be no secrets in these Highland communities. She wasn't ready yet to tell anyone the full story. There was no need for them to know she'd been about to be evicted from their city home. Lanrig had been a lifeline, which she'd grabbed with both hands. The excitement of the moving in, the children's delight when the pony turned up, even the little exploring expeditions they'd made since their arrival had filled them with eagerness to enjoy their new life.

Today had been a turning point. She'd come down to earth with a bump as she stood at the school gates and watched her children walk away from her. This was reality. The dwindling cushion of Lizzie's bequest wouldn't last much longer. She would have to find some kind of paid employment. And as for those two huge fields out there . . . how was she ever going to be able to work them?

Bethany put a hand on her shoulder. It was as though she'd read her mind. 'I think you're worrying too much, Hannah. No one expects you to become a crofter overnight. And you certainly don't have to work all this land. Lizzie never did.'

Hannah raised an eyebrow. Bethany was in her stride.

'Take the pasture out there, for instance. She leased that out for grazing. I don't expect she got much for it, but it would be a bit of easy income. You could do the same thing. And as for the field back there,' Bethany inclined her head towards the land on the other side of the track, 'well we all used to get involved with that.'

'You did? But how . . . ?'

Bethany laughed. 'It was Ross's idea. In her younger days, Lizzie had always planted out that field. She might have been a woman on her own but she was never afraid of hard work. Only, for the last few years . . . well, she just wasn't fit.'

'So how . . . ?'

'Like I said, it was Ross's idea. He rounded up all Lizzie's friends and neighbours — kids and all — and organised a tattie-planting day.'

Hannah stared wide-eyed at her.

Bethany went on.

'Some of the women took over Lizzie's kitchen to keep the sandwiches and hot drinks coming while the rest of us worked. It was great fun — and the tattie crop got planted in no time.'

Hannah was thoughtful. 'Sounds like a great idea.'

'Aye, and it worked just fine. We all came back later in the year to help with the harvesting, and everybody had a share of the crop. It was grand.' A spark of light came into Bethany's eyes and she snapped her fingers. 'Why don't you do that? Have a planting day, I mean. We could easily round everybody up again. I'll help you.'

'What?' Hannah shook her head. She was remembering the size of the field. 'I couldn't do that. For a start, I don't really know anyone here yet, certainly not well enough to ask them to put themselves out for me.'

Bethany tutted. 'You know Ewan and myself, and I've no doubt you've met Maggie and Jake Morrison.'

'Well, yes, but — '

'And there's Ross, of course. I'm sure he will want to muck in.'

The dour estate manager was the last person Hannah would ask to help her with something like this. She frowned. 'I don't think Ross Hunter would be as keen to help me as he was to help Lizzie.'

Bethany pursed her lips and stirred the tea Hannah had poured. 'You mustn't pay too much attention to Ross's manner. It's just his way. I think he feels uncomfortable around women he doesn't really know.' She glanced up, her eyes amused. 'Especially capable ones.'

'Oh for heaven's sake, that's ridiculous. How on earth would any of us survive if we weren't capable?' Hannah shook her head. 'The man liked Lizzie well enough, and by all accounts there was no more capable woman that her.'

'Aye, but there's a difference. Lizzie was old, you see, and therefore not a threat.'

'Threat?' Hannah's eyes widened.

'Hasn't anyone told you about his wife?'

Maggie had mentioned something about a divorce, but Hannah hadn't taken too much of it in.

'Ross met Louisa in Edinburgh. She was PA to some high-flying executive or other. By all accounts he was besotted with her. They married and he brought her back here to live in his lodge on the estate. The following year their son, Josh, was born; then things began to go wrong.' Bethany was warming to her story. 'Louisa was a city girl and never settled here. She hankered after her old life in Edinburgh — the smart clothes and the parties. She stuck it out for a few years, but she was never content. Eventually she just took off, taking their son with her. Ross fought her for custody of course, but the courts awarded that to Louisa.' She bit her lip, glancing up. 'That was about six years ago. The boy will be eleven now, just a year older than our Becky. Ross never talks about it.'

Hannah was remembering some of the things Maggie had told her. 'That must have been tough,' she said.

Bethany spread her fingers. 'Aye, Ross has had it hard, but it's still no excuse for his boorish behaviour, though.' Her voice softened. 'But . . . well, maybe it's easier to understand the way he is. Once you get to know him he is a really sweet man.'

It wasn't a description Hannah would have attributed to Ross Hunter, no matter how traumatic his past had been, but maybe she would give him a bit more rope. He had, she remembered, actually got on well with Robbie, Jamie and little Holly.

Bethany's voice cut into her thoughts. 'Tell me about your children. What do they think of Lanrig?'

Hannah sighed and looked around her. 'It's a lot for them to take in. They miss their friends, not to mention my parents.' She suddenly brightened. 'But Mum and Dad are coming up next weekend, so that will be something for us all to look forward to.'

Bethany touched Hannah's hand. 'Don't worry about the kids. They'll soon make new friends. Children do, especially now that they have started school. What age is your eldest?'

'Robbie's ten, Jamie's eight and Holly is just six.'

'Your boys are about the same ages as our two, then. Ewan said he would introduce them all to each other today. And of course, they're welcome to come down to the schoolhouse to play any time they like.'

Bethany was getting up to leave and Hannah realised she was sorry to see the woman go. Maybe the children weren't the only ones to be making new friends today.

Bethany turned as she reached the door. 'And remember what I said about the tattie-planting. Just give us the nod and we'll set the ball rolling.'

'Thank you,' Hannah said. 'I might just take you up on that.'

7

Hannah went outside after Bethany left and strolled out to the pasture. Seeing her approach, the pony stopped grazing and trotted over. She laid her cheek on the animal's silky coat and stroked its head. 'You're on our side too, aren't you girl?'

As though in response, Erin nuzzled into Hannah's shoulder, and the pair of them stood there gazing out at the river. A long-legged bird was wading in the shallows, jabbing its sharp beak into the water in search of food, but Hannah wasn't watching it. She was going over in her head what Bethany had said. Could she really go cap-in-hand to complete strangers and expect them to help her plant a whole field of potatoes?

She sighed, left the pony and walked around the side of the property, pausing to stare at the field. It looked bigger than ever today. The whole idea was fanciful; and anyway, wasn't September too late in the year to be planting anything except spring bulbs? She chewed her lip, thinking. Her dad was a gardener. He would know what kind of seed potatoes to buy — assuming she did decide to go along with Bethany's idea.

The obvious person to seek advice from was Ross, but she didn't want him thinking she was making use of people. The laird might be a better bet. Once she'd decided to drive over to the Big House, she felt better. At least she would be doing something.

As she pulled up outside Corrieglen House, Hannah vaguely wondered if Ross might be here. But there was no sign of him. The same sour-faced woman she'd met on her previous visit opened the door. And she didn't look any happier to see her this time.

'Do you have an appointment to see Sir John?'

'Well . . . er . . . no, but if he's busy I

can come back.' Hannah hadn't even thought of making an appointment.

'Who is it, Mrs Guthrie? Don't keep folks standing at the door.'

'It's the tenant from Lanrig,' the woman called back, keeping her eyes on Hannah. 'She hasn't got an appointment.'

'For goodness sake, woman. Since when did anyone need an appointment to see me?' Sir John was striding across the hall and waving his hand in a gesture of dismissal to his housekeeper. His annoyance turned to pleasure when he saw Hannah. 'Come in, dear lady, and tell me what we can do for you today.'

Hannah allowed herself to be ushered into the same room she'd been in before with Ross. The laird indicated a chair and settled himself opposite, steepling his fingers in a thoughtful gesture as he waited for her to begin.

She cleared her throat. 'The thing is, Sir John . . . '

He listened intently as she put Bethany's suggestion to him. When she had finished she sat back, waiting for his response. The old man's expression hadn't changed. Hannah bit her lip, looking away. She knew she shouldn't have come. It was a ridiculous idea. The local people all loved Lizzie, so of course they would have done anything they could to help her. She, on the other hand, was a complete stranger. What a cheek she had even suggesting this. She got to her feet, feeling the colour rise in her face.

To her amazement the laird waved her back down. 'You struck me as a smart, enterprising young woman the first time we met, and now I'm convinced of it.' He smiled. 'I think this is an excellent idea.'

Hannah stared at him. 'You approve?'

He nodded, smiling.

'Well, like I said, it was actually Bethany Stewart who suggested it — '

He cut in. 'And modest, too. I like that. It really doesn't matter whose idea it was. If you are prepared to set the wheels in motion, then you can count on my support. I'll get Ross to call out and see you. He's the one to advise you.'

'No, really . . . I think I can manage.'

'Nonsense, my dear.' The laird was standing up, signaling the meeting was over. 'That's what Ross is here for.' He led her to the door and took her hand, giving it a pat. 'I think you have the makings of a fine tenant crofter, my dear. I'm very pleased you decided to stay.'

As Hannah thanked him, the disgruntled Mrs Guthrie appeared from the shadows, making her suspect she'd been on the other side of the door listening to her conversation with the laird. She gave the woman her brightest smile and murmured 'good morning' as she swept past.

Hannah's heart was pumping as she got back into her car. It had gone so much better than she expected. Rallying the community to help her hadn't been part of her plan — not that she'd particularly had a plan. But if it all worked as well as Bethany suggested, then it would be wonderful.

She still had one reservation — Ross Hunter. What would he have to say about it all?

It was the next day before Ross's Land Rover appeared in the yard. Hannah was in high spirits. The children's first day at school had gone better than she had expected. She should have trusted Ewan and Bethany Stewart's judgment. Just as they had predicted, their children had made friends. She'd smiled as she'd watched her three offspring skip through the gate earlier without a backward glance.

Her heart did a nervous flip as she opened the back door to Ross. Why was she so wary of this man? The aroma of fresh coffee was filling the kitchen and she saw him sniff the air as he came in. Without asking, she turned and poured a second mug, pushing it across the table as she indicated for him to sit.

He cleared his throat. 'Sir John said you wanted to see me?'

'No, it was the laird's idea that you

should call by.' She swallowed. 'He thought you could help me with an idea that's been suggested to me by Mrs Stewart, the wife of the head teacher at Glenburn Primary.'

'I know who Bethany and Ewan are,' he said stiffly. 'And to save you any further explanation, I know what's been suggested.'

Hannah lifted an eyebrow. 'The laird's told you?'

Ross nodded. 'It shouldn't be too difficult to plant up that field. It's been done before.'

'Bethany said it was your idea to get the community involved to help Lizzie.' She could feel her colour rising. 'I suppose you think I have an awful cheek suggesting they might do the same thing for me?'

He frowned. 'Why would I think that? It's a sound plan. There's no point in leaving the ground lying dormant, even at this time of year.'

'You don't think it's too late to plant a potato crop?'

He leaned back in his chair and Hannah heard it creak under his weight. 'It's not ideal. A main crop should be planted out between March and May, but as long as the tatties are in before December they should be fine.' He reached for his coffee and was beginning to look quite at home in her kitchen. Hannah felt a tiny stab of victory.

'I'll check back at the estate, but I think we might have some seed tatties, although not enough to plant up the entire field. I'll order the rest. We should get a good discount.'

He'd said 'we', and it sent a warm glow coursing through Hannah's veins. Ross was looking more animated than she'd ever seen him. She put down her mug and looked across at him. 'I have a confession to make.'

His serious green eyes came up to meet hers. She swallowed hard again. 'I don't know the first thing about crofting . . . or farming . . . or gardening either, if I'm honest. That was always my dad's department.'

The mention of him sent pictures of home racing through her mind, scrolling through the happy times, like a newsreel. The little back garden of their Glasgow semi had been packed with vegetables every year when she was growing up. And her mother had never been short of a bunch of fresh flowers for the kitchen windowsill. When Hannah and Brian married, her parents had moved to a smaller city centre flat. It had no garden, so her dad took a plot on a nearby allotment. She smiled, remembering the boxes of produce that always accompanied her parents' visits. Alec Gilmore would be in his element planting a field of potatoes. The thought brought a happy glow to the pit of her stomach.

She realised Ross was still watching her, and there was a glint of amusement in his eyes. 'So you know nothing about crofting. That's quite an admission for someone who's just taken on the tenancy of a croft.'

Hannah straightened up, tilting her

head back defiantly. 'All I'm saying is that I'm going to need your help . . . well, probably more like advice. I'm not afraid of hard work, please don't think that, but I have three children to support and we can't live on fresh air — or the proceeds from a field of tatties.'

He was looking serious again, or was that understanding?

She took a breath. 'Look, I know it's going to take a massive effort to run this place — and I will do it. But I'll still need to find another source of income.'

Ross's brow furrowed. 'Lizzie used to sell the main part of her crop to a crisp factory in Dingwall. I don't know what they paid her, but I suppose it would all help. I'll try to track them down and you could give them a ring.'

Hannah's eyes lit up. 'That would be brilliant.' She paused, choosing her words carefully. 'I really appreciate your support. I'm determined to make a go of it here, I'm just not sure how much I have to do to keep the croft land up and running.'

Ross nodded and pursed his lips, considering. 'Pretty much what you seem to have planned anyway,' he said. 'If you wanted to lease out Erin's field for grazing, as Lizzie used to do, then I could have a word with one of the other crofters. I'm sure he'd be happy to put his cows back out there.'

'What about the pony? Wouldn't she be scared off by a field of cows?'

'Don't worry about Erin. She's used to it.'

Hannah cleared her throat. 'That would be very kind of you, Mr . . . er . . . Mr Hunter.'

'My name's Ross,' he said curtly, looking away. 'I could spread the word about planting out that field if you want a few folk out here to help you. Sundays are usually best for that kind of thing. Most folks hereabouts work on a Saturday.'

'Sunday's fine by me.'

'Right, I'll get things moving.'

She followed him to the back door and called after him as he reached his Land Rover. 'Ross.'

He turned to face her.

'My name's Hannah,' she said, smiling. 'Call me Hannah.'

His eyes narrowed, studying her for a second, and she thought she saw the shadow of a smile on his lips. Then he nodded, turning away to his vehicle again. She could see his black and white Collie leaping excitedly in the passenger seat at the approach of her master.

She closed the door and leant her back against it. She had a feeling they were all going to enjoy living at Lanrig.

8

There were two customers at the post office counter when Hannah walked in next day. They broke off their conversation to cast an interested glance in her direction. She nodded to them, smiling. 'Good morning.'

They smiled back, keeping an eye on her as they returned to their gossiping.

Maggie looked up and gave her a wave, then called across to the elderly woman waiting to pay for her groceries. 'I'll be with you in just a minute, Mrs McKenzie.'

The customer nodded, indicating she was in no hurry. Maggie slid her eyes towards the back of the shop. Hannah understood, hanging back until all the customers had been served before following her friend into the stock room.

One wall of the small, overcrowded

room was lined with shelves, sagging under the weight of tins and boxes. More cartons were stacked on the floor. A tiny table, covered in a bright red gingham cloth, had been squeezed up against the wall, along with two folding chairs. Maggie pulled one out, indicating that Hannah should sit as she reached for another cup from an overhead cupboard.

'No Jake today?' Hannah asked.

Maggie shook her head. 'He's gone to the cash and carry.' She reached over to feel the blue and white china teapot on the table. 'I brewed this ten minutes ago, but I think it's still hot enough.' She poured two cups and slid one across to Hannah, before sinking back in her chair with a loud sigh. 'I'm needing this.'

Hannah gave her a rueful grin. 'Tough morning?'

Maggie stretched her back. 'No more than usual. Pensions day is always a killer.' She took a sip of the hot tea and raised an eyebrow. 'You look like the cat that got the cream.'

Hannah laughed. 'I might not go that far, but maybe things are beginning to look up for me.' She corrected herself. 'For us.'

'Well, come on. Don't keep me guessing. What's this big news?'

Hannah took a breath and then launched into her story about Bethany's idea for the tattie-planting day. 'The laird is all in favour of it, although I don't think his housekeeper is all that happy.'

'Pay no heed to her. Jess Guthrie is a sour woman. And besides, this has nothing to with her. She's just jealous.'

'Jealous?' Hannah repeated incredulously. 'Why on earth would she be jealous of me?'

Maggie sighed and put her cup down. 'I suppose you'll find out sooner or later. She had Lanrig all lined up for her son, Gil.' She giggled. 'She wasn't expecting you to come along. None of us were. We didn't realise Lizzie had any relatives. What I do know, though, is that she definitely didn't want that Guthrie family taking over her cottage.'

'I see,' Hannah said, sitting back. 'Someone told me she'd had her eye on Lanrig. I suppose I just didn't expect her to be so bitter about not getting it.'

'I'm afraid Jess Guthrie will always find something to be bitter about, so don't you go worrying yourself about it, Hannah. If it wasn't this she was cross about, it would be something else. She's just a very dissatisfied woman.' She put her mug down. 'But enough of her. Your news is brilliant. It will be good to see a crop in that field again.'

Hannah leaned forward. 'Do you really think some of the locals will come along to help?'

Maggie nodded. 'Definitely.' She squinted up at the ceiling, calculating who might be approached. 'Well you can count on all of us for a start, and then there's Ross. Have you run the idea past him?'

Hannah's face lit up. 'He thinks it's great. In fact, he's offered to set the whole thing up for me.'

The shop bell tinkled, and Maggie rose wearily to her feet. Hannah glanced to the door. 'I could give you a hand in the shop if you like . . . at least while you're busy at the post office counter.'

Maggie pursed her lips. 'Well . . . '

Hannah took the hesitation as an acceptance. 'You can give me a crash course on how to operate your till.' She laughed. 'It can't be rocket science.'

'It is, actually. Just you wait . . . '

It was lunchtime before Jake got back, lifting an eyebrow when he saw Hannah behind the counter. 'A new assistant?' He smiled at his wife.

'Hannah's been lending a hand . . . and very good she's been, too.' Maggie sent a nod of thanks towards her friend.

'I don't suppose we can persuade you to do this again, on a more formal arrangement, of course?'

'What . . . you mean work here?'

'It wouldn't be a proper job, but I could offer a few hours if you were interested.'

Maggie and Jake were both looking at

her. Why not? She'd enjoyed the last couple of hours, and she could certainly use the money. 'If you're serious, then you can count me in.'

They both smiled and Jake disappeared through the back to put the kettle on again. Maggie crossed the shop to join Hannah. 'What kind of work were you doing in Glasgow? You never said.'

Hannah frowned. That life seemed like a million miles away from the little post office in Corrieglen. She took a breath. 'I was a kilt-maker.'

Maggie's eyes widened. 'You can make a kilt? You never mentioned that.'

Hannah nodded back, grinning.

'I could probably put some work your way, if you're interested,' Maggie said.

It was Hannah's turn to stare in surprise. 'Really?' She hadn't thought of taking on this kind of work up here, not with the croft being in such a remote place, but then why not? Her mind was racing through the possibilities. She would have to advertise, of course, and there was no need to take on more than just one or two commissions . . .

'The Abercrombies over at Inverbeg have a big wedding coming up.' Maggie bit her lip, trying to remember. 'And Ginty was talking about Gordon needing a new kilt.' She turned to Hannah. 'I could give her a ring, if you like . . . pass on your number.'

'Oh, Maggie, would you?'

Maggie flicked a hand, dismissing Hannah's gratitude. 'What are friends for?' she said, grinning.

An hour later, Hannah was waiting outside the school gates. So much had happened over the past couple of days. They had acquired a new member of the family in Erin, and plans were afoot to have their field planted out with a potato crop. Now, in the last few hours, she'd found a part-time job, and had the possibility of being commissioned to make a kilt. She felt like hugging herself.

'Someone at the door, Mum.' Jamie's voice carried down to the front room, where Hannah was putting away her sewing machine.

'I'll get it.'

She heard him clattering down the stairs and tried to reach the door before he did. But Robbie was already there. 'It's Granny and Gramps!

'Dad . . . Mum!' Hannah rushed forward, her arms wide. Breathlessly, she hugged each one in turn. 'But this is wonderful! We weren't expecting you 'til tomorrow.' She stepped back, looking wide-eyed from one to the other. 'Why didn't you phone?'

Hearing the new arrivals, Holly and Jamie pounded in to greet them.

'Come through,' Hannah laughed, drawing her parents into the warmth of the cottage, 'before we all squeeze you to death.' She guided them into the sitting room. 'We thought you weren't driving up until the morning.'

'Your father couldn't wait,' Peggy Gilmore said, throwing her husband a wicked grin.

Alec raised an eyebrow. 'I don't recall

you raising any objections.'

Hannah gave them another hug. 'What does it matter? You're here now. That's the important thing.'

Robbie settled himself on the carpet with a big grin on his face, while the others hurled themselves into their grandparents' arms again.

'Children!' Hannah scolded. 'Let Granny and Gramps get their breath back before you attack them.' She took their coats and they both sank gratefully into the comfy armchairs.

Holly immediately climbed up on Peggy's knee, and the boys perched themselves on the arms of their grandfather's chair.

'You should have phoned us first,' Hannah chided again. 'You must be exhausted driving all that way in the dark.'

'It was a last-minute decision, lass,' her father said. 'We just decided to throw everything in the car and get on with it.'

'Tell the truth, Alec. You didn't want

to miss out on any of the fun of this potato-planting thing.' She was glancing around the room as she spoke.

'Not bad for a Highland 'hovel' is it, Mum?'

Peggy's eyes widened. 'I never called it a hovel.'

But Hannah was laughing and wagging a finger. 'Yes you did.'

'What's a hovel, Granny?'

Peggy shot Hannah an embarrassed look. 'It's a kind of house . . . not nearly as lovely as your new house.'

'But you and Gramps have only seen this room.' Holly sent her mother a pleading look. 'Can I show Grannie and Gramps all the other rooms?'

'I want to show them, too.' Jamie leapt up.

'And me,' Robbie declared.

Peggy got up and gathered all three children into her arms. 'I think this is a job for everybody, and tomorrow maybe Robbie could show us around outside.'

Robbie's face lit up. He let the younger ones get on with the tour of the cottage. He'd been allocated the most important job.

Hannah went to fill the kettle, smiling at the sound of all the feet upstairs. She hadn't realised how much she missed her parents. They would make the most of these two precious days.

By the time they all trouped back into the kitchen, Robbie had set out mugs for the adults and three glasses for the children's bedtime milk.

'I didn't notice a spare room,' Peggy commented.

Hannah shook her head, reaching for the biscuit tin. 'I thought you could have my room. The bed's really comfy.'

'But where will you sleep, lass?' Alec asked.

'Oh, I'll be fine down here in the sitting room.'

Peggy tutted. 'We don't like turning you out of your bed, love.'

Hannah threw her hands in the air. 'I don't mind, Mum, honestly. We're all just so glad you could come.' She poured the drinks and set them on a tray. 'We'll be more comfortable through in the sitting room.' She carried the tray through and put it on the low pine coffee table as they settled themselves around the fire.

Peggy looked around the excited faces and decided that her daughter meant what she said.

Alec put his arm around Hannah's shoulder. 'You don't mind about us coming early, do you? It didn't make sense to leave the journey 'til morning. That would have given us hardly any time here.' He rubbed his hands together. 'And if there's a field of potatoes to get into the ground . . . '

Hannah gave her father a rueful smile. 'We didn't invite you here so we could use you and Mum for slave labour.'

Alec Gilmore shook his head. 'You call planting a few tatties slave labour?'

'It's more than just a few tatties, Dad. We have a whole field to plant out.'

'How many are coming to help?'

Hannah counted them off on her

fingers. 'Bethany, Ewan, Maggie and Jake. Then there's Ross, of course.'

'Ross?'

Hannah took another sip of her drink before putting the mug back on the table.

'He manages the Corrieglen Estate. He's organising this whole thing.'

'So it was his idea?' He gave his daughter a concerned look.

Hannah shook her head, explaining about Bethany.

Alec's brow knotted. 'Just so long as you're not being pushed into anything.'

Hannah got up and slid her arms around her father's shoulders. 'Nobody's pushing us into anything, Dad, honestly. The people here are really nice.' She paused, and Alec saw a slow smile twitch at her mouth. 'I really think were going to be all right here, Dad.'

Alec turned to Robbie. 'What's your part in all this, laddie?'

Robbie squared his shoulders, a glint of pride in his eyes. 'Same as you, Gramps. Becky, Rory, Jamie and I will all be helping to plant the tatties.'

'Friends from school,' Hannah interrupted.

Alec pursed his lips and nodded his approval. 'You've made some friends already? Well that's good.' He glanced at his wife. 'Isn't it, Peggy?'

The hesitation before her responding smile made Hannah frown. Surely her mother could see how well they had all settled in? She opened her mouth to speak, but her father got there first.

'So, how's all this planting business going to work then?'

Hannah forgot what she was going to say and outlined the plan for the next day. 'We'll be playing it by ear a bit, but Ross knows what he's doing, so I'm relying on him to organise things.'

'We've got a pony,' Holly cut in excitedly.

'A pony?' Peggy's voice lifted.

'We inherited her. Her name's Erin and she comes from a place called Eriskay.'

Peggy frowned. 'Another mouth to feed?'

'I don't think it's that bad. Ross says these ponies more or less look after themselves.' Hannah looked from one to the other, smiling. 'And I might be able to set up a little sewing business in the croft.'

'Now that sounds all right, doesn't it, Peggy?'

Hannah smiled at her dad — always the peacemaker.

'What kind of sewing business?' her mother asked.

'I've been commissioned to make a kilt for someone. And once word gets around that I can do this kind of thing . . . '

'Congratulations, Hannah. That's wonderful.'

Alec glanced at his wife. Of the two of them, Peggy had been the one most opposed to the move.

She'd been watching them all as they spoke. The children looked happy, and Hannah seemed to be carving out a new life for all of them. It wasn't what Peggy had expected to find. She'd been nurturing a secret hope that they would plead to come home with them. She sighed. But it seemed that this little croft house, with its fields and views and Highland air, was the place they now thought of as home.

Peggy looked up and saw Alec narrowing his eyes at her. She swallowed. He was right. Hannah and the children had a new life now — and she would have to accept that. She forced herself to smile. 'You're dad's right, Hannah. That's great news.'

'But that's not all,' Hannah went on excitedly. 'Maggie's offered me some part-time work at Corrieglen post office.' She sat back, smiling. 'You'll like her and Jake. You'll meet them on Sunday.' She reached across the table and touched her mother's hand. 'You'll love them, Mum.'

Now that she'd forced herself to accept that the family wouldn't be returning to Glasgow, Peggy found herself relaxing. Next morning she helped Hannah to prepare the food for the planters' Sunday buffet, while Alec busied himself finding odd jobs around the croft. The whole family had enjoyed a long, bracing walk across the fields in the afternoon.

Hannah was first to wake on Sunday morning. The first priority was to plug in the kettle. She never bothered closing the kitchen curtains, and looking out now she was surprised to see a black van parked in the far corner of the yard. Someone had arrived early. It was barely light.

Pulling a coat over her dressing gown, she went out and crossed the yard. Someone was in the driver's seat. She could see the tip of a cigarette glowing. Hannah tapped the window and it slid down. The man was in his mid-twenties. His dark, straggly hair gave him an unkempt appearance.

She cleared her throat. 'Can I help you?'

The dark eyes narrowed as his gaze skimmed unpleasantly over her. Hannah drew her coat closer. The stranger gave a slow smile. 'More like me helping you, Missus.' The accent was Highland, but the voice was harsh, with no sign of the soft lilt the rest of the locals had.

'I'm sorry. I don't think we've met.'

The van door was pushed open and the man got out. He was tall and scrawny, wearing jeans and a dark leather jerkin. His hand shot out. 'Gil Guthrie,' he said. 'The old dear said you might need a hand.' He nodded towards the field that had been earmarked for the potatoes.

Guthrie ... the laird's housekeep. This scruffy individual was her son! Nothing she remembered about the woman suggested she'd be extending any friendly gestures.

'You've come to help with the planting?' There was more than a hint of surprise in her voice. 'That's kind of you, but you're a bit early. We're not expecting the others for two hours yet.' She really didn't like the way he was looking at her. His grin was too close to a sneer.

He glanced towards the open kitchen door. Hannah's eyes narrowed. Was he expecting to be invited in . . . offered breakfast? With any of the other neighbours she wouldn't have hesitated, but not this man. She didn't trust him.

They both looked up as the beam of headlights swung into the lane. Hannah bit her lip. Another early arrival. But as the vehicle got nearer she began to smile. It was Ross! He pulled up alongside the van and jumped out.

'What are you doing here, Gil?'

Hannah could tell from his body language that he was less than pleased to see the young man.

Gil's shoulders went up in a careless shrug. 'Come to help with the planting. Why else would I be here?'

'Did Jess send you?'

Gil Guthrie's scowl was menacing. Hannah shivered.

'Well, thank your mother,' Ross said, keeping his voice even. 'But we already have more than enough people lined up. So we won't be needing you.'

Gil threw down his cigarette and stamped on it. He gave Hannah a long, appraising look before turning back to his van, and without a word he climbed in, slammed the door and took off at speed. They watched his taillights disappearing up the lane.

'You've made an enemy there, Mr Hunter,' Hannah said.

Ross's eyes were still on the retreating vehicle. 'You wouldn't have wanted him around, believe me.'

Lights were going on in the cottage bedrooms and Hannah turned, pulling her coat tighter. 'Come in and meet my parents. You can join us for breakfast.'

He hesitated, but Hannah was not accepting a refusal this time and gave him a little push towards the door. 'You can make yourself useful and brew some tea while I get dressed.'

He raised an eyebrow. 'Is that an order?'

She turned to grin at him. 'Please.' She heard him sigh as she ran up the stairs.

Judging by the voices she could hear as she quickly showered and dressed, Hannah guessed that the entire household was up and about. Her mother was setting the table as she came back into the kitchen, and her father was cutting bread.

Ross was at the Aga, a pile of plates warming by his side as he fried eggs in a pan and kept his eye on bacon under the grill.

Hannah's eyes widened. 'I didn't mean for you to cook the breakfast. I only meant . . . '

But Ross had turned, indicating she should sit. 'I'm good at this,' he said. 'You should make the most of it.'

Peggy raised an eyebrow, but there was a twinkle in her eye. 'Better do as he says, love. No point arguing with a man who cooks you breakfast.'

Hannah shot her mother a look. Peggy was smiling, and waved her down into a chair. Robbie, Jamie and Holly were already seated, and halfway through bowls of cereal.

Hannah put her hand to her head. Tendrils of damp hair were already escaping from the clasp she'd hastily clipped in. 'This is very kind of you, Ross, but you really didn't need to bother. I'm quite capable of cooking for my family.'

Ross turned, a tea towel slung over his shoulder, and placed a dish of grilled bacon and glistening sausages on the table. 'I've no doubt, but you should save your energy. There will be plenty of work for everyone before this day's out.' A fried egg had been put on each of the warm plates, and Peggy helped Ross put them on the table. 'There now,' he said. 'Bon appetite.' He was turning towards the door.

Hannah's eyes widened. 'Aren't you joining us?'

He shook his head. 'I've already eaten.' He squinted towards the window. 'Besides, I've a lot to do before we can get started.'

Hannah stared after him. She didn't see the look her parents had exchanged.

'What a nice young man,' Peggy said,

reaching for the toast.

Hannah shook her head, confused. Nice! There were many words she could have used to describe Ross Hunter. Nice wouldn't have been her first choice. But now she wasn't so sure.

Bethany and Ivan Stewart were first to arrive, their two children already running around the yard with Robbie and Jamie. Maggie and Jake turned up ten minutes later, with another man Hannah didn't recognise.

'This is Sandy Crawford. He farms the next croft to you.'

The man nodded shyly and accepted the hand Hannah offered.

'This is really kind of you, Mr Crawford. Is it you we have to thank for looking after Erin?'

'The pony was no trouble.' He looked out to the field where Erin was grazing. 'We're old friends.' He gave an awkward cough. 'I did it for Lizzie.'

'Well, we're very grateful to you. The children love her.'

'Aye, they would,' the old man said.

'And the name's Sandy.'

Hannah watched him as he limped away. He certainly didn't look very fit. Surely Ross wouldn't allow him to do any planting?

Maggie stepped in beside her. 'I can tell what you're thinking. Don't let Sandy deceive you. He ploughs a straight furrow.'

Hannah gave her a quizzical look.

'Sandy's the man with the tractor. We can't do anything without him.'

'He's brought his tractor?'

'You must have heard it wheezing down the lane.'

Hannah shook her head, laughing.

Another two couples she didn't know had arrived, and Hannah went to welcome them.

'I can't believe how kind everyone here is,' she said later to Peggy.

'They're certainly neighbourly,' her mother agreed, nodding towards the field, where the volunteers had organised themselves into a line and were dropping seed potatoes into the furrows ploughed by Sandy's tractor.

Ross looked up, wiping sweat from his forehead, as Hannah approached.

'I want to help,' she said.

He pointed to one of the far furrows the volunteers had not yet reached. 'You could start over there.'

She hesitated. 'I . . . err . . . I don't know what to do.'

Ross picked up a seed potato from the bag at his feet.

'Just cut it, like this.' He sliced through the potato, leaving a couple of buds on each slice. 'The trenches Sandy's ploughed are about six to eight inches deep. We're going along the rows putting a potato slice, cut side down, at the bottom of the trench, twelve to fifteen inches apart, and then covering them with about four inches of soil.' He squinted down at her. 'Think you could do that?'

She gave him a scathing look and headed off to find her box of seed potatoes. An hour later she'd planted a full row and most of the next when she stood up, a hand on her aching back.

'I should take a break now, if I were you,' Ross called from across the field.

Hannah glanced around her and was amazed to see that the planters were now more than a third of the way across the field. She cupped her hands round her mouth and shouted. 'I'll finish this trench and then get started on the food.'

Sandy twisted round in his tractor and gave her the thumbs up. Hannah waved back to him, laughing.

'I get the message,' she yelled against the wind.

Her mother was standing in the yard as she limped up, holding her back. 'I hope all this is worth it,' she said, giving her daughter a concerned frown.

Hannah smiled. 'It will be, Mum. I'm sure.'

Peggy nodded out towards the field. 'Your father's in his element. He's been looking forward to this since you phoned.'

'I didn't invite you here to work,' Hannah protested.

'I don't think your father would call

this work.' She pointed ahead, laughing. 'Look! They've even put little Holly to work.' Holly's jeans and bright pink wellies were totally encased in mud.

Hannah sighed, making to rush forward to rescue her daughter. But Peggy caught her arm. 'Maggie's looking after her. She's having a whale of a time and besides, I doubt if she could get any messier.'

They walked back to the cottage, arm in arm. 'I can see why you like this place.' Peggy paused to look around her. 'It's special.'

Hannah nodded. 'It weaves its magic on you.'

They hadn't gone back indoors, but instead had walked round to the front of the cottage and stopped, gazing across Erin's pasture to the river that was sparkling in the sun. Peggy's eyes were shining, and the idea came to Hannah in a flash.

'Why don't you and Dad move up here? You could easily sell your little flat in Glasgow and buy a cottage here.'

Peggy was taken aback. 'We couldn't do that. What would we live on?'

Hannah sighed. Her mother was right. Jobs were not easy to find up here. On the other hand, her dad was due to retire in a few years' time . . .

She'd planted the seed. It was up to them now.

Peggy checked her watch. 'Isn't it about time we put the finishing touches to that food?'

Hannah and her mother had set up trestle tables in the yard. By the time they had finished, the tables were laden with plates of sandwiches, home-made scones, shortbread and cakes. Sausage rolls were warming in the oven, and there would be bowls of homemade broth for those who wanted it.

9

'What a spread.' Bethany put a hand on Hannah's shoulder as her eyes travelled over the plates of food. 'You must have been baking all week to produce this lot.'

Hannah chewed her lip, her eyes scanning the table. 'D'you think they'll be enough?'

'I'd say there's enough here for an army. It's a veritable feast.'

Peggy came up as Bethany moved off to fill her plate. 'She's right, love,' she said. 'You've done them all proud.'

'*We've* done them proud. I couldn't have managed all this without your help, Mum.' She planted a kiss on her mother's cheek.

Peggy coloured and flicked her hand, dismissing the praise, but Hannah knew she was pleased. She turned, glancing around the yard for Ross. He was nowhere to be seen. Jake passed, and she caught his arm.

'Has Ross left?'

Jake took off his flat cap and scratched his head. 'Last time I saw him, he was out front making a fuss of that old pony of yours.'

Hannah strolled over to the pasture. Ross was in the middle of the field, ruffling Erin's mane as she nuzzled him with her nose. 'You've made a friend.' She came up, smiling.

Ross looked up. 'We're old mates, Erin and I. Aren't we, girl?'

Hannah slipped through the gate to join them. She patted the animal's back.

'She still misses Lizzie,' Ross said, looking out across the water to the far hills. There was sadness in his eyes, and she wondered if he was thinking of his son. She couldn't imagine how she would cope if one of her children was taken away from her. It was the first hint of vulnerability Ross had ever displayed, and she suddenly wanted to reach out and comfort him. She knew what loss felt like. Brian had let them all down, with his gambling and lying. But he'd been family, and even though Hannah had stopped loving him long before he died, she still missed him.

'You're miles away,' she said quietly.

Ross's head snapped up and he turned to face her. The sad, wistful look had gone. 'We're pretty much finished. The folks did a good job for you.'

She lowered her eyes. 'I rather think it was you who inspired them, not me.'

He looked at her with narrowed eyes, as though he was trying to see into her mind. 'Don't put yourself down, Hannah. People around here respect you.'

'None of it would have happened if it hadn't been for you. It was you who organised it all, rounded everyone up.'

'Method in my madness,' he said with a twinkle. 'It kept me out of the laird's way.'

Hannah raised an eyebrow. 'But he's a lovely man. Why would you want to avoid him?'

Ross frowned. 'A precious piece of

jewellery has gone missing and he's had everybody turning Corrieglen House upside down searching for it.'

'Jewellery? What kind of jewellery?'

'A Cairngorm brooch. It's been in the family for generations. Sir John kept in the desk drawer in his study so he could look at it every day.'

Hannah felt a cold hand grip her heart. 'What does it look like?' Her voice sounded strangely weak, for she already knew what he was going to say. She'd found a brooch like that in her car. It was tucked under the passenger seat. It was odd, but she assumed it had belonged to the car's previous owner, and had somehow been overlooked when the garage staff valeted the vehicle.

'It's a kilt sash brooch, the kind used to hold the shoulder plaid of Highland dress in place. This particular Cairngorm stone is one of the biggest ever known. It's embedded in a setting of silver thistles and it's very old and rare.'

'And valuable?' Hannah's voice was

hardly more than a squeak now. She'd thought the brooch to be a piece of worthless costume jewellery.

Ross tilted his head to look at her. 'It's irreplaceable.'

She cleared her throat. 'There's something I want you to see, Ross.'

He followed her back to the house and into the kitchen. She lifted down a small cane basket from a shelf and held it out to him. 'Is this the laird's brooch?'

Ross's eyes widened. 'Where did you find it?'

'It was in my car. I thought it must have belonged to the previous owner. I threw it in here, intending to contact the garage. I'd no idea it was valuable.'

Ross turned the brooch over in his hand and stared at it, his brows knitted. 'When was the last time you visited the laird?'

Hannah's eyes went to the ceiling. 'Umm . . . about a week ago, I think.'

'And when did you find brooch?'

'The next day.' Realisation suddenly dawned on her. But surely that couldn't be right ... could it? 'You think someone deliberately hid it in my car?' Her stare was incredulous.

'Maybe.' Ross's eyes were glinting with anger.

'But who would do that?' She shook her head. 'I don't understand. Why?'

'I could have a good guess,' he said grimly. He slipped the brooch into his pocket. 'I think you should be with me when I return this to Sir John. Do you think you'd be missed if you slipped away now?'

'Well, not now, Ross.' She waved her arms about her. 'I can't just walk out and leave everybody.'

Ross followed her gaze out of the window to where her helpers, their appetites now satisfied, had begun to drift into groups and were standing about chatting.

'Looks like the party's breaking up,' he suggested.

It didn't look that way to Hannah, and she certainly had no intention of hurrying any of them away. 'Why don't you go and grab some food while I get out there to thank everyone properly,' she suggested. 'And then, when they've all gone, I'll get Mum and Dad to look after the children and I'll go back with you to the Big House.' She saw him frown, but he nodded, and followed her into the yard.

It was an hour later when she eventually waved off the last of her friends. They'd done a magnificent job. She now had a small field of potatoes planted.

Jake offered to come back and give her a hand to tend the crops. 'I'll be looking for a sack of tatties, mind you,' he'd said with a twinkle.

'You deserve a lot more than that, Jake.' She linked arms with him and Maggie and walked them back to their car. 'I still can't believe how kind everybody's been.' She glanced at the newly planted field and felt the prick of a tear in her eyes.

Maggie gave her arm a squeeze. 'It's the Highland way, to help your neighbours.' She smiled. 'Don't worry, I'm sure you'll get your chance to return the favour.'

The Morrisons were last to leave. Her dad came to stand beside her as they waved them off. 'Ross tells us you have to see the laird. Is everything all right, Hannah?'

'Everything's fine, Dad.' She took his arm and walked back with him to the cottage, where Ross and Peggy were in the sitting room with the children.

'You've told them about the brooch?' Hannah asked Ross.

'I've left that for you to do.'

Hannah took a deep breath. 'You'll never believe this, but . . . '

Ten minutes later they were all still staring at her.

'You mean you found this priceless brooch and didn't mention it?' Peggy was shocked.

'Have you found treasure, Mummy?' Holly scrambled down from the sofa and began to dance around her mother.

'Sort of,' she said, ruffling the child's

silky hair. 'Mr Hunter and I have to go out for a bit.'

'Will the laird give you a reward?' Jamie's eyes were shining.

Hannah shook her head, laughing. 'I doubt that very much. But I think he will be very glad to get his brooch back.'

The sun was going down, streaking pink clouds across the big sky, as they drove up the lane. Hannah's head was full of questions. She stared at Ross's profile.

'So, are you going to tell me who did it? Who put the brooch in my car?'

He turned to her. 'Do I really need to answer that?'

'You think it was Mrs Guthrie?'

He nodded. 'Doesn't seem much doubt about it. That's probably why Gil turned up at Lanrig this morning. He certainly wasn't there to do you any favours.'

'You mean he might have been looking for the brooch?'

'Are you still locking your car at night?'

'Well no, not out here. I didn't think it was necessary. I mean, who's going to steal . . . ' The words trailed off as she stared at him. 'You think Gil was there to retrieve the brooch?'

Ross slid her a glance. 'More likely he was going to make a big show of finding it — at the same time putting you in the frame for stealing it.'

Hannah's hand went to her throat. 'That's horrible.'

'The thing is,' Ross sighed, 'what happens now? We've no proof it was the Guthries, and Sir John needs a house-keeper. Even if he believes us, he'll probably still take pity on the woman. The Guthries have been bleeding the old man dry for years.'

Hannah was shocked. 'Why has he put up with it?'

'Because he's a kind old man who doesn't like a lot of fuss.'

'Let's hope he sees sense this time and gets rid of the lot of them. Will Mrs Guthrie be here?' Hannah asked as they pulled up outside Corrieglen House.

Ross nodded. 'Probably. She's supposed to be here until eight. She cleans up after Sir John's evening meal.'

Hannah's hands shook as she got out of the vehicle. 'I'm not looking forward to this.'

'It's not you who has anything to worry about.' His face was grim. 'I can't say the same for the Guthries.' He rattled the heavy brass knocker and the big door swung open, revealing Jess Guthrie. Hannah caught the flicker of uncertainty in her eyes as she looked from one to the other. Ross brushed past the woman, taking Hannah with him.

'The laird is still having his supper,' Jess Guthrie called, hurrying after them.

Ross raised his hand to knock on the door to the laird's dining room, but it opened before he had the chance.

'Ross! . . . and Mrs Maxwell, too. Has something happened?'

The housekeeper was still hovering.

'We'd like a word, Sir John.' Ross half turned his head. 'In private.'

The old laird squinted at them from under white bushy eyebrows, before looking past them to the woman. 'That's fine, Mrs Guthrie. You can clear up later.'

Hannah scanned the half-eaten meal. 'We've interrupted your supper, Sir John.'

'You have,' he said sternly. 'So there had better be a good reason.'

Ross slipped his hand into his pocket and drew out the Cairngorm brooch. 'Mrs Maxwell found it.'

Sir John stared wide-eyed at them. 'You found my brooch?' He reached out, taking it from Ross's hand, turning it reverently in his fingers. He turned to Hannah.

'You found it? I don't understand. Where did you find it?'

Hannah gave an embarrassed little cough. 'In my car, actually.'

The laird stared at her. 'In your car? What was it doing in your car?

Ross stepped forward. 'Somebody put it there.'

The old man pulled out a chair and sank down on it wearily, letting the implications of the remark sink in. 'You're suggesting that someone in this household took my brooch and deliberately put it in this lady's car?' He looked up at them. 'For what reason?'

Ross shifted his weight from one foot to the other. 'I think we both know that, sir.'

'I see,' the laird said grimly. He stood up and gave Hannah a nod, but the sparkle had gone from his eye. 'I'm very grateful to you, Mrs Maxwell.' He turned to Ross. 'To both of you.'

There was no sign of Jess Guthrie as they left. 'She's probably skulking in the kitchens,' Ross said, his expression grim.

'Do you think Sir John realised what you were suggesting? I mean, will he know it must have been Mrs Guthrie who took his brooch?'

'He knows, all right.'

'What will happen now? Will he dismiss her?' She paused. 'Even if she was responsible, it's not as though she stole the brooch for herself.'

Ross stared at her. 'For heaven's sake, Hannah, the woman tried to make you look like a thief.'

'Does the family live in an estate cottage?'

Ross nodded. 'Jess and her husband, Duncan, have the tenancy of a croft on the other side of Corrieglen. But the laird could withdraw their rights over something like this.'

Hannah let out a gasp.

'There's no need to feel sorry for them.'

'But I do,' Hannah said quietly. 'I know what it's like to lose your home.'

She saw him frown. 'You lost your house?'

Hannah nodded, and felt her bottom lip tremble. They were on the road that ran alongside the river.

Ross pulled up and turned to her. 'I'm sorry, Hannah. I didn't realise.'

Hannah gulped back tears. She hated getting emotional. It was all in the past.

They had Lanrig now, and were already making new friends. Maggie had offered her work in the post office, and she had an order to make a kilt. But best of all, the children loved it here. They were so lucky.

She swallowed and told Ross her story. It was the first time she had ever talked about her life with Brian, and she left nothing out. She described his gambling problem, and the misery of the debt he left when he died. Ross listened in silence, but she saw his jaw tighten as she told him about the building society repossessing their home. When she'd finished he still didn't speak.

Hannah turned away. 'I'm sorry. I've embarrassed you. I don't usually burden people with my problems.'

'I'm not embarrassed,' he said quietly. 'I didn't realise you'd had such a bad time.'

Hannah bit her lip. 'That's all in the past now. I've moved on. We all have. We have Lanrig now, and I can't believe how lucky — ' But she didn't finish the sentence because tears were coursing down her cheeks. Just talking about the past had brought all the emotion to the surface. She swiped angrily at the tears. 'Sorry. I don't know what's got into me. I never cry.'

She had no idea how it happened, but suddenly she was in his arms. His hands were stroking her hair, fingers gently wiping away the tears. Then his lips brushed hers in the merest whisper of a kiss. It was a long time before they pulled apart.

Ross looked away, embarrassed. 'I shouldn't have done that. I took advantage. It won't happen again.' Without another word, he started the engine and drove back to Lanrig.

Hannah lay awake into the early hours. Why had she let him kiss her? It was all her fault. Telling him about Brian, then bringing on the tears. Ross probably took that as an invitation. She didn't know how she was going to face him again.

She edged back the duvet and got off

the sofa, padding across the room to open the curtains. It was still dark, but she could just make out Erin's pale shape moving about in the pasture. Her parents were going home this morning; it was another reason to feel depressed. They had only been at Lanrig for a few days, but she'd got used to having them around.

Unable to sleep, she crept quietly upstairs and took a shower, and then pulled on a pair of clean jeans and a thick blue sweater. She was in the kitchen making breakfast when her mother appeared.

'We're going to make an early start, love. Your father wants to avoid the traffic.'

Hannah reached for the cereal box in the cupboard and put it on the table. It wasn't what she wanted to hear.

'Wouldn't you be better waiting until the morning rush is over?'

Peggy began setting out the cutlery. 'If we leave it too long we might not want to go.'

Hannah spun round from the stove.

'Then don't. Don't go back to Glasgow. Stay here with us.'

Peggy began to smile, then she realised that her daughter was being serious.

'It makes sense, Mum. Why go home when we can all be together right here?' Even as she spoke, Hannah knew it was impossible. Her parents couldn't just pack in their jobs and move to a place where they had no financial support.

Peggy narrowed her eyes. 'Are you all right, love?'

Hannah could hear the concern in her mother's voice and swallowed. She forced a smile. 'I'm fine. I just wish you didn't have to go home so soon.'

They both looked up and saw Alec by the door. He came in and put an arm around Hannah's shoulders. 'We'll stay longer next time.' He smiled across to his wife. 'Won't we, Peggy?

Peggy nodded. 'In fact, I don't think you'll be able to keep us away. I really enjoyed working in that field with the others.'

Hannah could hear the children moving about in their rooms upstairs, and she called out for them to hurry. Holly arrived first, still in her pink dressing gown and dangling her teddy.

Peggy scooped her up. 'I think you need to get dressed, young lady.'

'Thanks, Mum. Tell the boys to hurry.'

They didn't, so breakfast was a rushed affair. Robbie was still chewing a piece of toast as they all gathered in the yard to wave Peggy and Alec off.

'I meant what I said, Hannah.' Alec hugged his daughter. 'We'll be back before you know it.'

Peggy bent down to plant kisses on three little cheeks.

'Ring me when you get home,' Hannah called after them, as the car pulled out of the yard.

There was snow in the air as she dropped the children off at school. She stood at the gate, glancing around for any signs of Ewan, and smiled when she saw him striding towards her.

'It was a good day yesterday,' he said. 'Bethany's still talking about that spread you put on.'

'It was the least I could do after all your hard work,' Hannah said. 'I don't know how to thank all of you.'

He shook his head, his eyes twinkling. 'No thanks needed.'

She turned to wave. 'Tell Bethany I'll call in when I get a minute.'

'She'll keep you to that,' Ewan called back.

Hannah took her time driving back to Lanrig. She wasn't looking forward to the emptiness of the place after everyone had gone. The last thing she expected to see was Ross's vehicle at the back door. Her heart was hammering in her chest and there wasn't a thing she could do to stop it.

Had he come to humiliate her, to accuse her of leading him on? Her hands trembled as she opened the car door and got out. He was striding towards her, his expression serious. 'All your visitors gone?'

She nodded, turning to open the kitchen door. He followed her in. 'I was going to have a cup coffee. Would you like one?'

Ross cleared his throat. 'Please.'

He paced around the kitchen, stopping by the window to look out at Erin's pasture. She sat down, casting around for something to say — anything that would ease the terrible embarrassment she felt.

But it was he who spoke first. 'It went well yesterday.' He still had his back to her.

'It was amazing. I still can't believe how hard everyone worked.' She put his mug of instant coffee on the table and pushed the sugar bowl towards him.

He swung round. 'I've come to tell you what happened about the brooch.'

Hannah waited.

'We were right to suspect Jess Guthrie,' he said, pulling out a chair and sitting down. 'She denied it at first, but it was so obvious that she was the one responsible that she eventually

185

broke down and confessed to the whole thing.'

Hannah shook her head. 'I still don't understand. Why did she put it in my car?'

'She wanted you to get the blame. She's mean and vindictive — and Gil isn't much better. That's why he was at your place on Sunday.'

Hannah looked up and caught the challenging green eyes watching her. For a split second their gaze locked, then Ross looked away. 'He was here to find the brooch and return it to the house,' he said, narrowing his eyes at the view from the window. 'Except that he never would have returned it. I know Gil. He would have pocketed the brooch and told his mother he couldn't find it.' Ross drained the last of his coffee. 'It's worth a couple of thousand on the open market.'

Hannah sank back in her chair and let out a long sigh. 'So what happens now? Is the laird going to evict the Guthries?'

Ross shook his head. 'That's exactly what he would be doing if I had any say in the matter. But no, he's let them off with a warning.' He shook his head. 'He should have reported it to the police.'

Hannah put her hands to her head. 'The Guthries will blame me for all of this. Jess has been hostile from the start. The woman just doesn't like me.'

'You know why, don't you?'

'If you mean about Lanrig — '

'Jess wanted Lanrig for Gil,' Ross cut in, giving an incredulous laugh. 'As if the laird would have allowed that. Not that he needed to worry about it, because Lizzie left the tenancy to you.' He met her eyes again. 'It's in safe hands now.'

Hannah felt herself colour at the unexpected compliment. But Ross was already on his feet and heading for the door.

10

Hannah was smiling as she put the phone down. One kilt order wouldn't make her a fortune, but it was a start. The last kilt she'd made had been five months earlier, and it hadn't been her best effort. The customer, a nice man who had lived three streets away from their home in Glasgow, said it was excellent, but she could tell by his expression that he'd expected better. There hadn't actually been anything wrong with the kilt, but it wasn't up to Hannah's usual high standard.

The eviction had been hanging over her then, and she feared for her family's future. But that wasn't her customer's fault. Feeling guilty, she had knocked ten per cent off the price and told the man that she had miscalculated. That wouldn't happen this time. She glanced across the room to her sewing corner.

This kilt would be the best she had ever made.

The rush to get the children off to school after her parents left hadn't given Hannah time to tidy the kitchen. The breakfast dishes were still in the sink. She picked up the mug Ross had drunk from. He hadn't mentioned that kiss. He was pretending it never happened — and that was what she would do, too.

She glanced out to where the pony was grazing. Jamie had pleaded with her for a dog, but pets had been the last things on Hannah's mind over the past few months. The pony was different; looking after Erin had seemed like the one thing she could do for Lizzie, a tiny show of gratitude for the new life they'd been given.

She left the dishes and wandered outside. The animal's delight at seeing her sparked a little stab of pleasure. They were going to be just fine now. She was sure of it.

Hannah was smiling as she drove into

Corrieglen. It was mid-morning and the usual queue had formed at the post office counter. Maggie was too busy to notice her arrival, but Jake, on the shop counter, gave her a wave. 'There'll be a lull soon, if it's Maggie you've come to see.'

'No problem,' Hannah called back. 'I'm not in any hurry.'

He came over to join her. 'We usually have a cuppa at this time of the morning. Come through and have a sit down.'

He led the way to the storeroom and filled the kettle at the tiny sink. 'We can't match that spread you put on yesterday,' he said over his shoulder, grinning. 'But there's a packet of biscuits around here somewhere.'

Hannah spooned coffee granules into the mugs Jake laid out. He was pouring on the boiling water by the time Maggie appeared. 'Thanks for coming, Hannah,' she said, collapsing into the chair her husband had vacated. 'So when can you start?'

Hannah laughed. 'Are you that desperate?'

Maggie glanced up at Jake. 'Well, he is, aren't you?' She gave him an indulgent grin. 'Jake can't wait to be free of all this.'

Hannah put out her hands and shrugged. 'When do you want me?'

'The post office counter is busiest midweek, say Tuesday through to Thursday, and probably from nine to around twelve or one o'clock.' She looked up. 'Could you manage that, Hannah?'

'I'll have to drop the children off at school first, but I could come here straight after.'

Maggie smiled and pumped Hannah's hand. 'Consider yourself hired.'

Jake reached for the kettle again. 'I think this calls for a top-up.'

Hannah sensed as soon as she stepped into the kitchen that afternoon something was wrong. It was nothing she could put a finger on, just a feeling. She stood in the middle of the room and looked around. What was it? Had someone been here while she was out? She wondered briefly if Ross had a key, but surely he would never let himself in without her permission?

She checked around the sitting room, picking up books and toys the children had left lying around. It wasn't as though they had anything worth stealing. Even her sewing machine was second-hand, and worth very little to anyone else. She couldn't see anything out of place and decided she must have imagined it.

Today had been a triumph. She had had an enquiry about a kilt which she was sure would turn into a definite order, and a little part-time job at the shop which would bring in some much-needed cash. There wasn't much left of Lizzie's bequest. It would still be a struggle making ends meet here in Lanrig, but she could make it work. She was sure of it now.

She spent the next hour going through the books and swatches of tartans. She would be confident and knowledgeable when she went to measure Gordon Abercrombie for his kilt. The order wasn't yet certain, but Hannah was confident that by tomorrow evening she would be making kilts again.

Inverbeg, where the couple lived, was more of a hamlet than a village, having only three properties that Hannah could see. She got out of the car and knocked on the cottage door. Ginny Abercrombie opened it.

'Spot on time.' She smiled, ushering Hannah into the tiny front room. A roaring fire was throwing out a terrific heat and Hannah wondered how safe it was for the two huge leather armchairs to be so close.

'This is the lassie Maggie telephoned about. The one who's going to make your new kilt, Gordon.'

Gordon Abercrombie looked up, his round face glowing from the heat, and eased himself out of his armchair. 'Well, lass?' He patted his bulging stomach. 'D'you think you can do anything with me?'

Hannah gave him her brightest smile

and reached into her bag for her tape measure.

Fifteen minutes later they had decided on a 13-ounce pure new wool medium-weight ancient Abercrombie tartan. Their friends' wedding was to be in a month's time. Hannah explained that it could take a few days for the fabric to arrive, but assured them the kilt would be ready.

Her face was flushed with excitement when she arrived back at the croft. The children were in their pyjamas. Robbie and Jamie were cross-legged in front of the fire; Holly was on Maggie's knee as she read them a story. But they all scrambled up as Hannah came into the room. Maggie smiled across at her. 'From the look on your face, I'm guessing it went well.'

'It went more than well.' Hannah's eyes were shining. 'I have my first kilt order.'

'Well, congratulations,' Maggie said, getting up and crossing the room to put her arms round Hannah's shoulders.

'I don't want to count my chickens,' Hannah said later, when they'd settled the children in bed and were having a cup of tea in front of the fire. 'But I'm hoping this is just the start, Maggie.'

'Tell me about your job in Glasgow.'

Hannah nodded. 'I worked for a big Glasgow kilt-maker for five years. The money wasn't great, but I got the training I needed to take on some extra private work at home.' She got up and poked the fire, reaching to put another log on the embers. 'Word soon got round that I could provide the same quality of kilt for a fraction of the price of a shop-bought one.'

Maggie raised an eyebrow. 'Didn't your employers have something to say about that?'

'They might have, if they'd known about it.' Hannah shrugged. 'We needed the money.'

'Didn't your husband work?'

'Yes, but he earned peanuts. You can't pay a mortgage and feed and clothe three children on peanuts.'

It was the first time Maggie had ever heard a sour note creep into Hannah's voice. She studied her friend's face as she gazed into the fire and saw the hurt in her eyes. She and Jake had such a comfortable life in comparison to what Hannah's must have been like. They worked hard in the shop, certainly, but it was satisfying because they were at the heart of the community.

Sensing Maggie's eyes on her, Hannah glanced away, embarrassed. She hadn't meant to sound so bitter. It wasn't Brian's fault that he had been in a dead-end job. The most frustrating thing was that he never seemed to mind. He had no ambitions to better himself. Maybe if she hadn't been prepared to work so hard for both of them, then Brian might have taken on a bit more responsibility.

'Are you all right, Hannah?' Maggie had reached out a hand to her, and she realised her cheeks were wet with tears. This was happening too often now for Hannah's liking. She supposed it must be a delayed reaction, but it had to stop! She wiped her wet face with the back of her hand. 'I'm fine, really I am. What must you think of me?'

'I think you are a very brave young woman, and a lovely mother to those three little ones upstairs.'

Hannah could feel her eyes filling up again. 'I don't usually do this. It's just that everyone here has been so kind to us.'

'And why wouldn't they be? You're in the Highlands now, lass. You're one of us.' Maggie stood up and patted Hannah's hand. 'If I don't make a move, Jake will be sending out the search parties.'

Hannah got up and helped the older woman on with her coat before strolling with her across the yard to her car. 'Thanks for tonight,' she said quietly.

Maggie waved away her gratitude. 'Your wee ones are a pleasure to look after.

'I didn't just mean the babysitting.'

'I know what you meant, and there's no need for thanks,' Maggie said, climbing into her car before turning to give Hannah a wistful smile. 'You and Lizzie would have got on just fine, you know.'

There was already a line forming at the post office section as Hannah walked in next morning. Maggie glanced up and waved her through. A few of the customers' faces were familiar and Hannah nodded a greeting.

'Am I pleased to see you,' Jake said, moving aside to make room for her behind the grocery counter. 'This lot will all be moving over here in a minute and we'll be busier than that big supermarket over in Dingwall.'

Hannah glanced across at the queue. There were no more than half a dozen customers, but they filled the tiny shop. She smiled. 'I think I'll manage.'

'Well, I'll stay until you're sure you've got the hang of things.'

'There's no need, Jake. I'll be fine. You've shown me how to work the till, and if there are any problems I'll just ask Maggie.'

Jake gave her a searching look. 'Well

. . . if you're sure. It's just that I promised I would call in at Sandy's. His old tractor's been playing up and I said I would stop by.'

'So why are you still here?' Hannah grinned, shooing him off.

The next hour passed in a flash. Hannah wasn't exactly rushed off her feet, but there was always someone needing to be served. It was eleven o'clock before she was able to take a breather. Maggie disappeared into the back kitchen and returned five minutes later with two mugs of instant coffee and a plate of biscuits on a tray. 'Sustenance for the workers,' she said, putting the tray on the counter. She picked up one of the mugs and took a few sips. 'I needed this,' she gasped, before looking up at Hannah. 'So, how are you today? Jake, the old devil, just dropped you in at the deep end.'

'I'm absolutely fine, Maggie . . . more than fine. I'm really enjoying this.'

Maggie dipped a chocolate digestive into her coffee. 'Right enough, if you want to know everybody's business then this is the place to be.'

'You're a wicked woman, Maggie Morrison.' Hannah's eyes were twinkling.

'Speaking of other folks' business, did you know Ross's son, Josh, is coming to stay with him?'

Hannah put down her mug. 'I didn't,' she said slowly. 'He never mentioned it.'

'No, he wouldn't. Likes to keep his business private, does Ross.'

'So how . . . ?'

'Jess Guthrie mentioned it. If you want your business spread all over the Highlands, then Jess is the one to tell.'

'When's he coming?'

'Next weekend, as far as I know. Ross is driving down to Edinburgh to collect him.'

Hannah frowned. 'It's not the school holidays or anything.'

'Oh, he's not coming for a holiday. According to Jess, he's moving up here permanently. Louisa has got herself a job in Canada apparently, and Josh doesn't want to go with her.'

There had been no time to ponder this news because three customers came in at once and Maggie headed back to her counter.

It was lunchtime before Hannah got the chance to think any more about Ross's son. She tried to remember what Bethany had told her, but the only thing that stuck in her mind was that Ross had wanted, and failed to get, custody of his son. And now the boy was to live with him. Surely that must be good news?

The bolt of tartan Hannah had ordered for Mr Abercrombie's kilt arrived on Thursday. When the children were in bed she worked late into the night cutting out the fabric and pinning the pleats into shape.

Friday was her free day from the shop, and she spent the time working on the kilt. She'd been worried that she might have lost her touch after all the stress of the past months, but she'd learned her skills well and was soon engrossed in her task.

It was mid-afternoon when Hannah heard her name being called. She looked up, frowning. Someone was in her kitchen. She hadn't heard a vehicle approach, but then she'd been so concentrated on her work that a pipe band could have passed right by her window, unnoticed.

'Sorry. I did knock, but — '

Hannah sprang to her feet, her hand at her throat. 'Ross! I didn't hear you come in.'

His big frame filled the doorway. He gave her a sheepish grin. 'This is a terrible imposition, but I have to go away for a day or two . . . '

He didn't finish the sentence, glancing down at the black and white Collie, who was thrashing her tail against the doorframe.

'The thing is . . . Tess is due to pup next week.' He gave a helpless shrug. 'I don't trust anyone else to look after her.'

Hannah's eyes flew open. 'You want me to be her midwife?' Her voice rose in a squeak.

He laughed. 'Of course not. Like I said, her litter's not due for another week. I just wondered if you could keep an eye on her until I get back tomorrow?'

Hannah chewed her lip, looking down at the dog's swollen middle. Why hadn't she noticed the dog's condition before? 'Oh, I'm not sure. What if it happens sooner?'

Ross fished into his pocket and produced a scrap of paper. 'I've written down the vet's name and number, but I'm certain you won't need it.' He stepped closer. 'I don't want to ask Sir John. He's inclined to panic. And I can't leave poor Tess at the mercy of Jess Guthrie.'

Hannah sighed. He had a point. And besides that, he was probably going off to collect his son. She bent to ruffle the dog's long silky coat. 'Looks like it's you and me then, Tess.' She looked up at Ross. 'Until the master gets back.'

She thought for a moment that Ross was about to throw his arms around her, but he didn't. Instead he took a step back. 'I'm very grateful,' he said quietly.

'Have you brought her basket and food and stuff?'

He nodded. 'It's all in the vehicle. I'll just fetch it.' He turned, leaving the dog to gaze up trustingly at Hannah. Seconds later he was back, his arms full of Tess's things.

'Put the basket down there, by the Aga,' Hannah instructed, 'where it's nice and warm.' She'd told herself she wouldn't ask where he was going. It was none of her business. But the words were out before she could stop them.

Ross raised an eyebrow, and at first she thought he was going to ignore her question, but he didn't. 'I'm going to Edinburgh to collect my son, Josh. He's coming to stay with me.'

Hannah saw the delight in his eyes and smiled back at him. 'You never mentioned you had a son. Will he be staying long?'

'For good, I hope.' The delight had

turned to a glint of cold steel. Ross would make sure his son was here to stay.

There was so much Hannah wanted to say, to ask, but she forced herself not to. He would tell her what he wanted her to know. When he made to go, she followed him to the door and waved him off before turning back to Tess with a sigh. She had settled herself in her basket, but there was a definite glint in her blue eye.

Hannah raised an eyebrow. 'Don't you dare have your puppies tonight,' she said.

11

Hannah suspected Tess wasn't going to last until next week, as Ross had said. There had been a restlessness about the dog that prompted Hannah to warn the children about not making too much of a fuss of her.

'Ross has had to go away for a day or two, and he's left Tess for us to look after,' she'd explained as she drove them home from school.

Robbie gave a whoop of glee and punched the air.

'We've got a dog?' Jamie's voice rose to a squeal.

'No,' Hannah said firmly. 'We're looking after her, that's all.'

'Can we play with her in the yard?'

Hannah shook her head, laughing. 'Well, let's just see how Tess feels about that, shall we? Her puppies will be due soon and she may just want to sleep.'

There were more whoops of delight from the back seat. 'Cool,' Holly said. 'Will we see the puppies, Mummy? Can we play with them?'

Hannah sent up a silent prayer that there would be no unexpected arrivals before Ross returned.

She knew something was happening by the way Tess was pacing restlessly around the kitchen. The children sensed it, too, and kept their distance.

'Is Tess going to die, Mummy?' Holly asked tearfully, as Hannah tucked her up in bed that night.

'No, darling. Tess is not going to die. She'll be just fine. In fact . . . ' She stoked her daughter's cheek. 'She might have a surprise for you in the morning.'

Tess delivered her first puppy at ten minutes to midnight, closely followed by numbers two, three, and four. The event hadn't been nearly as traumatic as the buildup, and Hannah's help had not been needed. She watched, entranced as each new life came into the world and Tess tended her little family. It was after one a.m. when she wearily trudged up the stairs.

Keeping the children's excitement in check was her main priority next morning. Tess and her brood were still cosy in their basket when the three of them tiptoed into the kitchen.

Hannah laughed. 'You can take a peek, but don't touch the puppies.'

Holly dropped to her knees and gazed into the basket. 'What shall we call them?'

Robbie rolled his eyes. 'We can't give them names, silly. They're not our puppies, are they, Mummy?'

Hannah gathered the three of them around her. 'They belong to Ross,' she said gently.

Jamie frowned. 'No they don't. The puppies belong to Tess. She's their mother.'

'Well, yes . . . but.' Hannah ruffled her son's hair. 'Maybe Ross might let us name one of them.' It was the least he could do under the circumstances, she thought.

'Puppies!' Maggie's voice on the phone was a mixture of shock and amusement as Hannah related the dramatic happenings of the previous night. 'Ross had a bit of a nerve expecting you to look after his dog, even if he did have to collect his son.'

'To be fair, Maggie, he didn't know this would happen. The pups weren't due until next week.' Hannah sighed. 'And Tess was Lizzie's dog, after all. I suppose I was doing it for her.'

'So when does Ross get back?'

'Not sure. Sunday at the latest, I think. But that's not the reason I'm ringing.' She paused, screwing up her face. 'I'm looking for advice. I don't know anything about looking after dogs, let alone puppies.'

'You don't have to look after them. That's Tess's job. Just let her get on with it. She'll get up for her food when she's hungry, and let you know when she wants out. So long as they are warm and dry and comfortable they will be just fine.'

'Thanks, Maggie.'

'Can I call in to see them?'

Hannah laughed. 'You're worse than the children. Of course you can. We'll look forward to seeing you.'

'How are you getting on with Gordon Abercrombie's kilt?' Maggie asked, reaching for one of the shortbread fingers that Hannah offered as they sat at the kitchen table.

'Another week should do it. There's a lot of hand stitching in the finish.'

'Your phone will be ringing off its hook once folk around here know what you can do.'

Hannah glanced at Tess's basket, where the four pups were suckling contentedly. 'One or two more orders just to keep things ticking over would be great.'

The Abercrombie order had come at the right time. Any way of increasing the family income would be welcome. It was certainly cheaper living at the croft than it had been in the city, but she still needed to earn more money.

As though she had read Hannah's thoughts, Maggie reached into her bag and drew out a brown envelope. 'Your wages.' She smiled, handing it over. 'I should have given it to you before you left on Thursday. I'm a rubbish employer.'

Hannah's face lit up. 'Believe it or not, I'd forgotten all about this. Thanks, Maggie.'

It was late morning next day when Hannah heard the sound of Ross's Land Rover in the yard. She'd been stirring a pot of broth on the Aga and put the spoon down to go and open the door. He wasn't alone. The boy who scrambled down from the passenger seat looked about Robbie's age. His hair was thick and blond, and his eyes the same clear green as his father's.

'This lady is Mrs Maxwell. She's been looking after Tess for us.'

Hannah shot out her hand. 'Call me Hannah.' She smiled.

'Josh,' the boy mumbled shyly.

'Very pleased to meet you, Josh.' She

bent down to whisper in his ear. 'We have a surprise for you.'

He gave her an unsure look, but she took his hand and led him into the warm kitchen. His eyes lit up when he spotted the basket. 'They're here, Daddy. The puppies are here!'

Ross came in behind them and his mouth curved into a smile. 'Well, I never.' He squatted down beside the basket and stroked Tess's head. 'You clever old girl.'

Hearing the voices, Robbie, Holly and Jamie came running through, and stared with interest at Josh. Hannah introduced them.

'Have you come to take Tess and her puppies away?' Holly asked sulkily.

Ross got to his feet, glancing at Hannah. She shrugged. 'We'll have to think about that,' she said.

'Is Josh staying for lunch, Mum?' Jamie asked.

Ross was about to raise his hand to refuse when he caught sight of his son's hopeful expression.

'Of course they're staying,' Hannah cut in. 'Now why don't you take Josh through to the front room to watch that film we recorded yesterday?' She hustled all four of them out of the kitchen and turned to Ross. Her cheeks were glowing from the heat of the oven and a wayward strand of dark hair had fallen across her forehead.

Ross had to resist an urge to step closer and gently smooth into place. He glanced away, embarrassed at the thought, and then turned his attention to Tess and her new little family. 'Which one would you like?' He looked up and saw her startled expression. 'Well, you did help to bring them into the world. It's only right that you should have your pick of the litter.'

Hannah sat down, an uncertain smile twitching the corners of her mouth. 'First the pony, and now this.' She nodded towards the basket. 'You seem determined to supply us with a menagerie of animals.'

'Well they do kind of belong at

Lanrig. Lizzie doted on this little Collie. But if you don't want one of the puppies . . . '

Hannah went to the basket and crouched down to stroke the soft coats. 'I didn't say that.' She turned and met his vivid green stare. For a second neither of them spoke. The connection she felt with this man was electric. She forced herself to turn away, hoping her shaky legs wouldn't buckle under her. The croft kitchen wasn't small, but his presence in it was overpowering.

'Can I help?'

'Help?'

Ross swallowed. 'I meant with the cutlery.' There was a slight tremor in his voice. 'I could set the table . . . get the plates.'

The sound of the children's laughter drifted through from the other room. 'Actually,' she said, pushing the straying lock of hair from her face, 'you could go through and supervise that lot, if you really want to make yourself useful.'

Ross glanced at her, and Hannah saw

the slight narrowing of his eyes. He thought he was being dismissed.

'And then you can come back and pour us both a glass of sherry. It's in that top cupboard.'

His frown turned to a grin and he crossed the stone floor. She heard his voice mingling with those of the children and smiled. They were enjoying themselves.

There was a sparkle in Ross's eyes when he returned and headed straight for the sherry cupboard. He lifted down the bottle and found a couple of glasses. 'It's good to see Josh having fun.'

'Didn't he have much fun in Edinburgh?' Hannah hadn't wanted to probe into Ross's private life, but if he wanted to talk about it, she wasn't about to stop him.

'His mother is a very busy woman.' He sighed. 'I suppose it can't be easy looking after a child on your own when you have to go out to work.'

Hannah sipped her sherry. 'Tell me

about it,' she sighed.

Colour crept into Ross's face. 'Sorry, that was a stupid thing to say. No one knows more about the struggle to bring up kids on your own than you, Hannah.' His eyes were on her again. 'Louisa's not half the woman you are,' he said quietly.

The words were out before had time to consider the implications. He was making a fool of himself. He drained his glass and stood up, carrying it to the sink, and stood with his back to her. 'Josh wasn't happy about leaving Corrieglen in the first place, but Louisa insisted that he would have a better life with her. I fought her for custody, but in the end the court sided with the mother.' His shoulders rose in a sigh. 'You can't imagine how much it hurt to lose him. I felt my world was falling apart.'

Hannah leaned forward. 'I can understand that,' she said quietly.

He turned, giving her a searching look. 'Yes, I think you can.' He looked away again, and Hannah saw the muscles in his jaw contract.

'She never settled here, you see. Louisa is a city girl. She needed the fashion boutiques and restaurants, the museums and supermarkets. Walking the country tracks or taking off into the hills never appealed to her. All she could think of was getting back to Edinburgh.' He shook his head. 'I can't imagine why she would assume that was the kind of life our son would want.'

There was silence between them for a moment, but now that Ross had started to confide in her, she didn't want to interrupt him.

He cleared his throat. 'I hardly saw Josh after Louisa took him. She could always find an excuse for putting me off. I think she was worried that if Josh came back to Corrieglen for a holiday, he would want to stay.'

Ross was staring at a spot on the far side of the kitchen, and Hannah knew he was back in the past, re-living the painful memories. 'Louisa had custody of Josh,' he continued. 'I had access rights, yet she was still determined to keep me from seeing my son. Well, I'd had enough. I threatened to take the whole thing back to the courts.' He gave a grim smile. 'Fortunately I didn't have to. The threat was enough to make her see sense, and things were better after that. Louisa agreed to Josh coming to Corrieglen during the school holidays.' He glanced up, as though suddenly realising that Hannah was still in the room, and smiled. 'I have full custody of Josh now. There were just a few papers to sign before Louisa flew out to her new life in Canada.'

Hannah's dark eyes were bright with anger. She couldn't stay quiet any longer. 'Louisa was prepared to just abandoned Josh?' She struggled to keep her voice from rising.

'Not abandon, no. Louisa loves Josh. She would have taken him with her if she'd got the chance, but he kicked up such a fuss about going that she was forced to contact me. This is the arrangement we've reached, and as far as I'm concerned, it's the best one.'

'What about Josh? Is he happy with this . . . arrangement?' She stressed the word.

Ross looked up, a quizzical expression on his face. 'You've seen him. Doesn't he look happy?'

Why was she getting involved in this? It was none of her business. And Ross was right; the boy certainly hadn't appeared to be unhappy. Hannah put up her hands. 'I'm not criticising, and you're right, Ross. Josh looks very happy to be here. I'm just urging caution, that's all. It's not any easier for a single dad to bring up a child.'

Ross was staring down at his feet. Had she said too much? She went over to him and touched his shoulder. 'I'm only saying, don't try to do it all on your own.' Her voice was soft. 'We're all here for you . . . if you need us.' Hannah looked up into his face and when their eyes met she saw the tenderness there. His fingers traced the outline of her jaw.

'I might be taking you up on that,' he said.

They drew apart guiltily at the sound of approaching feet. 'Is lunch ready yet, Mum? We're all starving.' It was Robbie.

Holly appeared behind him, her head nodding vigorously. 'We're all starving,' she repeated.

Hannah laughed, nodding in the direction of the stairs. 'Take Josh up to the bathroom, and all of you wash your hands.'

Holly's face screwed into an indignant scowl and she held her chubby fingers out for inspection. 'But they're clean,' she whined.

'Wash them anyway,' Hannah said, turning her daughter to follow the others.

'Can I help dish up?' Ross asked. It was as though the moment they'd shared only seconds before had never have happened.

'I thought you'd never ask.' She put

on her brightest smile and pointed to the cupboard where the plates were kept.

The meal wasn't grand: roast chicken, roast potatoes, carrots and broccoli, with a huge dish of baked rice pudding to follow. Hannah looked around the table as the children tucked into their food. Even Josh seemed to be enjoying it.

After lunch, when the dishes were washed and stacked back in the cupboard, Ross made a move to leave. Hannah noticed the children's long faces. Josh tugged at his father's sleeve.

'Can we take Tess and her puppies home with us, Daddy?' His voice was pleading.

Robbie and Jamie exchanged distressed looks and Holly flew across the room to Hannah. 'They can't take the puppies . . . tell them, Mummy. The puppies are ours.' Tears were filling her huge blue eyes and beginning to roll down her cheeks.

Hannah drew her close. 'The puppies don't belong to us, Holly. They belong to Tess — and she lives at Josh's house.'

'But they like being here,' Holly whimpered.

'They do all look quite cosy,' Ross said, lifting an eyebrow at Hannah. 'And this kitchen is much warmer than the one at the lodge.' He crouched down beside his son. 'What do you think, Josh? Shall we ask Hannah if Tess and her puppies can stay here until they are a little bit bigger?'

Josh gave a reluctant shrug. He wasn't happy, but he could see the sense in this. He turned doleful green eyes on Hannah. 'Could I come and visit them?'

Hannah bent down and gave him a hug. 'You can come any time at all, Josh.' She turned to the others. 'Can't he, children?' They all nodded enthusiastically.

Hannah followed them out, and felt the cold blast of approaching winter as she opened the door. Ross turned.

'Sorry, I rather forced your hand there. Do you mind keeping the pups for a little longer?'

She shook her head. 'I would have suggested it, anyway. And the same goes for you, by the way, Ross. Call by anytime.'

For a second Hannah thought he was going to kiss her again, but he touched her arm instead. 'Thank you . . . for everything,' he said quietly.

Hannah nodded as he turned to put a hand on Josh's shoulder before crossing the yard to their Land Rover.

Word of Tess's puppies spread fast in Corrieglen and the new arrivals were creating quite a bit of interest. Ross was spoilt for choice deciding which of the local families who'd inquired would provide the best homes for them.

In the end he decided to offer Maggie and Jake one of the puppies, and Ewan and Bethany at the school would have another. They would keep the third puppy for Josh.

'How long before we can take him home?' Maggie asked as she sat in Hannah's kitchen the following week-end.

'Ross doesn't want them to be separated from the mother until they are around ten weeks old.'

Maggie rolled her eyes up to the ceiling as she calculated. 'That would be around mid-January, by my estimation. They'll be a real handful for you by then.'

'Ross has offered to take them all back to the lodge.' Hannah wrinkled her nose. 'But they're settled here now. It would be a shame to move them.'

'You're too soft, my girl,' her friend chided.

'They're part of the family now. We've never had so many visitors.'

Maggie looked up, her eyes serious. 'You're not feeling so lonely any more, then?'

'I have a house full of children. How could I be lonely?'

'I just thought you were missing your folks for a while back there. You seemed pretty depressed after they left. Jake and I were worried about you. It can't have been easy to uproot your family from their life in the city and come to a place like this.'

Hannah eyed the older woman, and the kitchen chair creaked as she moved. 'Do you read cups as well?'

Maggie sniggered.

'But you're right,' Hannah admitted. 'I did feel a bit like a fish out of water when we first moved in.' She put out a hand. 'Don't get me wrong, Maggie. I love this place. People here have been so good to us — you and Jake, especially. You've been a real friend, and you gave me a job. You even pointed me in the direction of that first kilt order.' She smiled. 'Did I mention that I've had two others since then?'

Maggie shook her head, her eyes widening. 'No . . . really?'

Hannah put down the mug of coffee she had been nursing and smiled. 'We should be able to manage, if I can keep the orders coming in. But there's no getting away from the fact that I do still miss my parents . . . we all do. Mum and Dad would jump at the chance of moving up here, but I can't see that happening.'

'Why not?'

Hannah shrugged. 'It's not practical. Oh, they could sell their place in Glasgow, and probably have enough for a deposit on a small cottage around here, but they would still need an income.'

Maggie sighed. 'I suppose you're right. I can keep an eye open if you like. I usually get to hear of things first.'

Hannah smiled. 'Thanks, Maggie, I would appreciate that.'

But in her heart she knew there was no possibility of her parents ever being able to move to Corrieglen.

12

Josh was in Jamie's class at school, and over the next few weeks the two had become great friends.

Ross had protested when Hannah offered to collect Josh from school with her own children. But she'd soon convinced him that it was the ideal arrangement if Josh was to keep up with the puppies' progress. And having another mouth to feed at teatime was hardly going to stretch her budget.

The first snow came at the beginning of December. Hannah noticed the powdery flakes as she drove to the post office. 'Do you think it will last?' she asked Maggie, casting a worried glance to the heavy sky.

Maggie followed her gaze and pouted. 'This stuff won't lie.'

She'd been right. By mid-morning the flakes had stopped, and a watery sun was beginning to emerge. Not that Hannah had much time to enjoy it; being Friday, the shop was extra busy. Things had eased off by lunchtime and the two women sat in the back room, warming their hands around mugs of hot coffee.

'How's the multi-tasking going over at Lanrig?' Maggie asked, popping her favourite chocolate digestive into her mouth.

Hannah raised an eyebrow. 'Which particular task are you referring to?'

'The puppies, of course. They must be quite a handful now that they've got so big. You must spend your day mopping up after them.'

Hannah laughed. 'Actually, it's not that bad. Ross has built a temporary enclosure in the yard so they can get out and run about, without running off.'

'Ah yes, Ross. Quite the handyman these days.' She squinted at Hannah. 'I know it's none of my business, but are you two . . . ?'

Hannah's blue eyes widened, and she shook her head, tutting. But Maggie had noticed the twinkle. 'You are such a nosey old biddy,' she chided. 'Ross and I are just good friends. He only comes over to check on the dogs, and to collect his son.' She knew their friendship was fanning the fires of local gossip, and much to Hannah's embarrassment, one of the customers at the shop had even told her what a lovely couple they made.

But they weren't a couple. While Hannah struggled with her growing feelings for Ross, he seemed more determined than ever to keep his distance. Since he'd told her about his ex-wife, and the struggle he'd had for custody of Josh, there had been no more confidences. She wondered if he now regretted that conversation.

'Well if you say so,' Maggie said. 'Sometimes relationships just need a bit of a push.'

'There *is* no relationship, Maggie. I told you.'

'Well, the man's a fool then. That's all I can say.'

Hannah knew her friend had only her best interests at heart, but speculating about a non-existent romance between her and Ross really didn't help. She was glad when the shop bell tinkled again, and the conversation was interrupted.

The pale sun had given up its struggle to shine and had retreated again behind a bank of black clouds. By two o'clock it was snowing again.

Maggie sighed, peering out at the whitening road. 'Maybe I was wrong. This snow could get a lot heavier.'

Hannah's mobile trilled in her apron pocket and she answered it. 'Thanks, Bethany, I'll be right over.'

Maggie's face was anxious. 'Is everything all right?'

'Just a precaution. They're worried over at the school that this snow might get worse. Ewan and Bethany are ringing round the parents to collect the children early.'

'Quite right,' Maggie said. 'I'll manage here. You get off, Hannah.'

'Well, if you're sure.' But she was

already heading for the back room to grab her coat.

They were all back at the croft before the real snow began to fall. The children tumbled out of the car amid squeals of delight.

Holly grabbed Hannah's hand. 'Let's make a snowman, Mummy.'

The others had bounded into the kitchen, dumping schoolbags as they went. 'Can the puppies come out to play with us?' Jamie pleaded. 'Please, Mum?' The pups were already prancing excitedly around the kitchen.

'They have to go outside anyway, so I don't see why not. But only for five minutes.'

Hannah was almost knocked over in the rush of dogs and children when she opened the back door again. Tess was fighting a losing battle to control her exuberant pups. The wind had picked up and the big snowflakes were being thrown up against the back wall of the cottage. She took a final look back, smiling at the children's snowball fight;

and satisfied that they could come to no harm, she went inside to ring Ross and reassure him that Josh was with them.

His number was engaged, but he'd probably know by now that the school had closed early and that she would have collected Josh with the others. She stood up, shaking her head at the pile of abandoned rucksacks that littered the floor, and began tidying up. The snow was becoming a blizzard. Hannah went to the back door.

'Right, everyone inside now,' she called.

There were a couple of half-hearted objections, but she suspected they'd all had enough. The four children trudged back to the house, kicking the snow from their boots at the back door as she had instructed them. The dogs still looked as though they were enjoying themselves, but the little faces were covered in snow, and even Tess was beginning to look concerned.

Ten minutes later, dogs and children were warm and dry again, and all looking for food. Hannah was dishing up homemade fish fingers when Ross rang.

'Josh is fine,' she said. 'The children are all just having tea.'

'The snow's been drifting. I can't get out to the croft, Hannah.'

She could hear the anxiety in his voice. 'Don't even think about trying to struggle out here. Josh can sleep with Jamie tonight.'

'Are you sure, Hannah?'

'Well, of course I am. Josh will be quite happy with us, and you can collect him in the morning.' She paused. 'Are things really bad out there, Ross?'

'A few of the smaller roads are blocked, which is why I can't get through to Lanrig. It will probably have sorted itself out by morning.'

Ross had been right and the weather had eased up overnight. They were all still at breakfast when he arrived.

'Daddy!' Josh flew out of his chair and into his father's arms. 'Jamie and Robbie and me are going to build a snowman. Will you help us?'

Ross looked at Hannah, and she gave a helpless shrug.

'Only if Hannah agrees to join in.' He grinned, keeping his eyes on her.

'Do I have a choice?' she asked, laughing.

Ross swung round to face the children. 'What do you say, kids? Do you want Mummy to help us?'

They all screamed, 'Yes!'

'I'd say the ayes have it.' He grinned, turning back to Hannah.

It hadn't snowed any more during the night, but it was still four or five inches deep in Erin's paddock. Hannah was glad she had taken the animal into the shelter of the barn.

Only the occasional snowball flew through the air as the six of them worked on the big, fat snowman. An hour after they started, they all stood back to admire their work. Sammy the snowman, with his red woolly hat, carrot nose and toothy smile made out of stones, was magnificent.

'Can we stay out a bit longer, Mummy?' Jamie was putting on his most persuasive voice.

'You can, but not for much longer,' Hannah said. 'It's getting very cold out here.'

Ross followed her back into the cottage, where the puppies were playing a game of tag around the kitchen. 'I think it's time this lot came back to the lodge with me. You can't move in here for dogs.'

Hannah sighed. 'Five of them are a bit of a handful,' she admitted. 'They're all so lively.'

Ross crouched down to them, and the puppies immediately began jumping all over him. He laughed, trying to keep his balance. 'Yes, I definitely think I should take them back to the lodge.'

Hannah had put the kettle on and was setting out mugs and biscuits.

'There's all hell to pay back at the Big House,' he said. 'The laird has lost another one of his most prized possessions. It's a diamond necklace

235

this time, that's been in the family for generations.'

Hannah raised an eyebrow. She knew what Ross was thinking, but surely Jess Guthrie wouldn't risk losing her job a second time? 'I'm sure it will turn up. He's probably only mislaid it.'

'Yeah, right,' Ross said. He was obviously not convinced.

They hadn't noticed the sky darkening, or that the snow had started again. They both looked up as Holly burst into the kitchen, her woolly hat and coat covered in snow. Her little round face was red with indignation. 'They won't let me go with them, Mummy. Why can't I go with them?' She stamped her foot and a clump of snow fell off her boot onto the kitchen floor.

Hannah frowned. 'Go with them where, Holly? Where have they gone?' She was already on her feet and heading outside. Ross followed.

The snow was falling hard now, and Hannah's heart was beginning to pound. She couldn't see the boys anywhere. She wheeled round. 'Ross! Where are they, Ross?' Her voice was rising. 'We have to find them.'

Holly began to cry. Hannah was wading frantically through the snow. Ross caught her arm. 'I'll go. They can't have got far.' He squatted down to Holly's height. 'Show me which way the boys went, Holly.'

Huge tears were rolling down Holly's face. Hannah put her arms around her. 'You're not in any trouble, sweetheart. Just tell Ross which way the boys went.'

Holly lifted her arm and pointed towards the river. An icy hand gripped Hannah's heart and she raised her eyes to Ross. His grim expression was no comfort.

'I'm going after them. You stay here with Holly. I have my mobile phone and I'll call you as soon as I catch up with them.'

They hurried after him, back to the cottage. Sensing the adults' fear, Holly began to wail, rubbing her eyes with her tight little fists. 'Are Jamie and Robbie lost, Mummy?' she whimpered.

Hannah was struggling to fight back her own tears of panic. But now was not the time to fall apart. She had to stay strong for Holly.

Ross's arms came around them both. His voice was gentle, reassuring. 'They can't have got far. I'll find them.'

The snow was falling so heavily now that the river had disappeared from view. What if they had fallen in, stumbled in, unseeing in the blizzard? Hannah put her hands to her head. This was a nightmare.

Ross was throwing on his padded jacket, pulling on his gloves.

'Should we call the police?' Hannah's voice was numb.

'Give me twenty minutes. If you don't hear from me, then call them.' He squeezed her arm as he went out.

They watched him trudging through the snow. The swirling whiteness had long extinguished any trodden paths across the fields. Hannah bit her lip. Ross couldn't do this by himself, no matter how well he knew the terrain.

She rang Maggie, and heard her gasp of shock when she told her the boys were missing. Then her friend drew in her breath. 'Right, this is what we do,' she said. 'You telephone the Big House, Hannah. Tell Sir John we need as many people as he can muster out there searching. I'll try to get some of the menfolk from the village to join them.' She glanced out at the swirling snow and grimaced. 'I'm closing the shop. Jake and I are coming right over.'

'But the roads must be blocked by now, Maggie! Don't put yourselves in danger.'

'Ach, a bit of snow never stopped us. We'll all be there. Don't you worry.'

'Thank you, Maggie.'

Hannah's hand was shaking when she clicked off the connection and punched in the number for the Big House. It was ten minutes before her mobile rang again. She grabbed it, her heart pounding. 'Ross! Have you found them? Are they all right?' The split-second hesitation before he spoke told her everything. 'You haven't found them, have you?'

'Not yet, but we will.' He was forcing a confidence into his voice he didn't feel.

'They've been gone almost half an hour, Ross.'

He could hear the tremble in her voice. She was right to worry: the conditions had worsened and even he, who knew these hills so well, was becoming disorientated. 'I've rung the police,' he said quietly. 'And they have called out the Mountain Rescue Team. The Air Sea Rescue helicopter will join us just as soon as the visibility allows.'

'I rang Maggie. She and Jake are coming over. They're rounding up a search party. The laird's also contacting people he knows to help us . . . ' She broke off, breathless.

'The rescue services have suggested a rallying point. You can let the others know we will be meeting at the far end of Sandy Crawford's land, at the bend in the river.'

The mention of the river sent another chill down Hannah's spine. 'What else can I do, Ross?'

'You've done well, Hannah. Once all these people get here we should find the boys in no time.'

'You really think so?' Her voice was hardly a whisper.

'We'll find them . . . I promise you.'

Hannah put the phone down and glanced round at Holly. She'd fallen asleep on the sofa. Tess and her pups were curled up in front of the fire, tired out after their romp in the snow. She reached to touch Holly's soft pink cheek. 'Ross will find them, my precious,' she whispered. 'They'll all be back soon.' The tears were rolling unchecked down her cheeks. She watched the clock, mesmerised by the methodical click of the second hand. She didn't hear the thump on the back door at first, but the callers were not waiting to be invited in.

'It's only us,' Hannah,' Maggie called. 'We've got Ewan and Bethany with us.'

Hannah rushed into Maggie's arms,

and then reached for Bethany. 'Thank you all so much for coming.' She glanced back to the phone. 'There's still no news.' She saw Jake and Ewan exchange looks. 'Ross is meeting the police and mountain rescue people at the bend in the river.' She shrugged. 'Does that mean anything to you?'

Both men nodded. 'I'll pass that word round,' Ewan said, turning to Jake. 'We'll take my four-by-four. It'll be easier going.' They gave Hannah a final nod and headed back out.

'I think a cup of tea is in order,' Maggie said, turning to fill the kettle.

Bethany led Hannah back to the sitting room, where Holly was beginning to stir. They stood at the window, staring out at the falling snow.

'The children were so excited when it started. We built a snowman . . . look.' Hannah's voice shook. She pointed out to the pasture. The snowman hadn't been visible fifteen minutes earlier, but now she could see it clearly. 'Is it my imagination,' she said, 'or is the snow beginning to ease off?'

Bethany narrowed her eyes and gazed out across the paddock. 'I think you could be right.'

Hannah clasped her hands. 'Please, God. Make it stop snowing.'

Holly was awake, rubbing her eyes, struggling to sit up. Maggie came back with a tray laden with coffee and biscuits, and a glass of juice for Holly. She smiled down at her. 'I'm glad you're awake, young lady, or you'd have missed the biscuits.' Holly forgot about how upset she'd been earlier, and smiled back.

Bethany touched Hannah's hand. 'You look exhausted. Shall I take Holly upstairs?'

Hannah managed a weak smile. 'What do you think, Holly? Would you like to show Bethany your toys?'

Holly looked from the plate of chocolate biscuits to Bethany's smiling face. It was a difficult decision.

'Tell you what,' Bethany laughed. 'Let's take the goodies with us. We can have our own little picnic upstairs.'

Holly clapped her hands and let out a little squeal of delight, before turning to her mother. 'Will Jamie and Robbie and Josh be back when we come downstairs again?' The look of trust in Holly's eyes made Hannah's lip tremble.

'I hope so, darling,' she said softly.

Ross, too, had noticed the weather was easing up. He'd reached the muster point and was listening for any sound of approaching vehicles. The police were first to arrive. Ross counted ten bright yellow jackets making their way towards him.

'I'm Sergeant Jim Campbell,' the ruddy-faced policeman said, pumping Ross's hand. He nodded behind him. 'The others aren't far behind. Now, sir, if you can just tell us what's happened?'

Ross squinted impatiently into the still-falling snow. They were wasting time. 'We have to get out there, searching.'

'We'll do that more effectively when the mountain rescue team arrive to co-ordinate things.' He looked up, pointing to the figures trudging over the hill. 'This looks like them coming, now.'

Sir John also turned up with a contingency of estate workers and more men from the village. Ross recognised all of them.

It seemed like a lifetime, but it could only have been minutes before the sergeant re-appeared, having taken instructions from the leader of the mountain rescue team. He told the volunteers to fan out across the field and call out if they found any clues to the children's whereabouts. The police contingency was concentrating on the river.

An underwater search team would be brought in later if this initial search proved fruitless. Ross shivered at the thought of that last plan. The boys were alive . . . Josh, Jamie and Robbie were alive! They had to be!

The snow was almost knee-deep in parts, and still the searchers struggled on. Some had had the foresight to bring sticks with them. Others broke off frozen branches from the trees. The hills and fields Ross knew so well were now a vast, white alien landscape — and there was still no sign of the boys.

'We've come too far,' Ross said, rubbing a gloved hand over the icicles of snow caking his eyebrows. 'They're just small children. They could never have made it out here.'

The leader of the mountain rescue team narrowed his eyes, scanning the white fields. 'I think you're right, Mr Hunter,' he said with a sigh, his eyes straying to the river. Ross followed his stare and felt his heart freeze over. He shook his head, unwilling to consider the possibility that was being silently implied. Josh was NOT in the water. Robbie would have looked after him and Jamie. He hadn't got his son back after all these years only to lose him again.

He thought of Hannah back at the cottage. At least he was out here doing something. She could only wait — and waiting was the worst part.

Over at Moraig croft, Sandy Crawford was pushing back the covers and swinging his feet onto the floor. The bedroom was freezing. He pulled on the thick tweedy dressing gown he kept on a hook on his bedroom door, and struggled into his slippers to pad downstairs.

He made a poor invalid at the best of times; but now, with the snow thick on the fields outside, he felt even more depressed than ever. He filled the kettle and cut himself a hunk of bread and cheese. He had intended to take it back upstairs, but the kitchen felt more comfortable than his cold room. He'd stoked up the fire in the range that heated his water and kept the downstairs cosy.

He frowned at the snow. He knew he would have to check on the pigs at some time. There was no point putting it off. While the kettle boiled he eased his long grey coat over his dressing gown, pulled on the green rubber boots he kept by the back door, and ventured out.

The barn where the pigs lived was at the far end of the yard, and he muttered bad-temperedly to himself as he struggled through the snow. Then he stopped, listening. What was that noise? He stood very still. There it was again! A kind of whimpering. *Please don't let it be one of the pigs*, he thought. The last thing he needed right now, in this weather, and in his poor state of health, was a sick animal.

He reached the barn door and lifted his hand to unlatch it, and then stared. It was already open! He gave it a push and it creaked as it swung back.

'Hello! Is anyone in there?'

He heard a rustling of straw and his heart began to thud. He wasn't up to dealing with an intruder. What if there was a gang of them?

'Come out, I say.' He tried to sound masterful . . . confident. But even he could hear the tremor in his voice.

There was a movement in the corner of the barn. Sandy reached for the spade by the door. 'Well . . . come on!'

He brandished the dirty spade. 'Show yourself!'

There was a movement in the corner. 'We didn't mean to trespass,' a little voice said. 'We just came in out of the snow.' Robbie stepped uncertainly out of the shadows, followed by a wary Jamie, and then Josh.

Sandy stared at the three frightened little faces, and his mouth dropped open. 'My heavens! How long have you boys been here? You all look frozen to the marrow.' He shook his head in disbelief at them. They were hardly more than babies. What were they doing out here, and in this weather?

Robbie opened his mouth to explain, but no words came. Instead, to his horror, huge tears slid down his face.

'Oh, my goodness. Come away out of here. We'll hear the explanations later. There's a fire in the kitchen, and you three look like you could do with thawing out.'

They followed the old man back along the track he had made in the snow, and into the warmth of his croft house. Sandy peered at the three waif-like youngsters and raised an eyebrow. 'Don't I know you two? You're the laddies from Lanrig.'

Feeling more confident that the old man wasn't angry with them for sheltering in his barn, Robbie stepped forward. 'I'm Robbie Maxwell, and this is my brother, Jamie.' He pulled Jamie forward, then turned to point at Josh. 'And this is Josh Hunter.'

Jamie's bottom lip quivered. 'We got lost in the snow.' He rubbed his wet eyes with his fists. 'We want to go home now, please.'

Sandy poured tea into four big mugs and heaped sugar into all of them before tipping in the milk. 'Sit down and drink this. It'll warm you.' He pushed three of the steaming mugs towards the boys. 'And I'll have a look for that phone number your mother gave me when we did the tattie-planting that day.'

The mention of their mother and home was beginning to cheer them up.

'You were the man with the tractor,' Robbie said.

Sandy nodded. 'Aye, that I was.' He looked at Josh. 'You'll be Ross's son, then?' Josh nodded. 'Well, I suppose I'd better ring him, too.'

Hannah stared at the clock. The boys had been gone for almost three hours. She got up and paced the room for the umpteenth time. 'Why don't they ring, Maggie? Why doesn't Ross ring? They must have found them by now.'

Maggie got up and went to put an arm around Hannah's shoulder. 'It's only been ten minutes since Ross last checked in. And look . . . ' She turned round to look out of the window. 'It's stopped snowing. Now that has to be a good thing.'

Hannah sighed. 'I'd better go and check up on Holly. Bethany can't keep her amused forever.' She turned to go when her mobile rang. She tore across the room, snatching at it. She didn't recognise the number.

'Yes?' It wasn't one of the search

team. 'Oh, it's you, Sandy.'

Maggie could hear the disappointment in her friend's voice. She wasn't interested in neighbourly chats; not today.

'Actually, Sandy, do you mind if I ring you back later? I'm keeping this line free.' Hannah's eyes suddenly flew open. 'What! And are they all right?'

Maggie jumped up. 'Have they turned up? Has Sandy found them?'

Hannah's eyes, bright with tears of relief, gave her the answer. The two women hugged. 'Where did you find them, Sandy? Are you sure they're not hurt or anything?'

She heard a sigh at the other end of the phone. 'To answer your first question, the three of them were tucked up in my barn, keeping my pigs company. And as for the second question, well decide for yourself.' He handed the phone to Robbie.

'Mum? Can you come and collect us? Mr Crawford's made us tea, and he opened the box of shortbread he was keeping for Christmas. But we'd like to come now.'

Hannah swallowed, unable to speak. Tears were coursing down her cheeks. Maggie gave her shoulders a squeeze. 'Didn't I say they would all be fine?' she said, but there was a tear in her eyes, too.

Hannah had a thousand questions, but the explanations could wait. It was enough that her boys, and Ross's son, were safe.

Sandy came back on the line. 'Can you ring Ross and tell him I've got his boy here, too?'

Hannah took a long, shaky breath. 'It will be my pleasure, Sandy.' She glanced at Maggie, her eyes brimming. 'Ross will be there to collect the boys in no time. And, Sandy . . . thank you so much.'

Hannah clicked off the connection and punched in Ross's number. 'The boys have turned up,' she said breathlessly when he answered. 'Sandy Crawford found them in with his pigs.'

'Thank God.'

She could hear the relief in Ross's voice. She swallowed. 'Can you collect them?'

For a second he didn't answer, and she knew he was swallowing back emotion. Then he said, 'I'm on my way.'

It was almost an hour before the kitchen door burst open and the three boys rushed in. Ross was still outside, stamping the snow from his boots. Hannah threw her arms wide and gathered all three into a hug. She could feel the prick of tears behind her eyelids again, but she was determined not to cry in front of them. She let them go, stepping back, hands on her hips. 'Well, you boys have had some adventure.'

'You said we wouldn't be in trouble.' Jamie tilted his head and put on his coaxing expression.

Hannah gave them a teasing scowl as she helped them out of their wet jackets. 'There's a pot of chicken soup simmering away on the range, and an apple pie warming in the oven.' Three pairs of eyes lit up. 'But I want you all in the bath first.'

'Does that include me?' Ross came into the kitchen with a grin that split his face from ear to ear. Their eyes met for a long moment, neither of them trusting themselves to speak. Then Hannah smiled.

'Thank you, Ross,' she said, in a voice so quiet he had to strain to catch the words.

13

News of the boys' safe return was a cause for celebration in Corrieglen. So many people wanted to pass on their good wishes that Hannah's phone had hardly stopped ringing. Even the minister at the tiny church in Glenburn had called and told them he would be offering prayers of thanks in his next sermon.

But best of all, Hannah's parents were on their way. She hadn't told them about their grandsons' little escapade until it was over and the boys were safely home. But it hadn't lessened the shock.

'Your dad and I are driving up there right away.'

'Mum, as much as we would all love to see you, it really isn't necessary. The roads are bad and you have your jobs to think about.' She was trying to sound as reassuring as any dutiful daughter should, but her fingers were crossed that her mother would ignore the words. She desperately wanted them to come.

'Forget the jobs. There are plenty of others who can take over in an emergency.'

Hannah gave an unsure laugh. 'The emergency is over, Mum. The boys are home and safe now.'

'It doesn't stop your father and me wanting to make sure of that for ourselves.'

'Well . . . if you're sure . . . '

'Dad's on his mobile right now checking out which roads are passable. We might have to come the long way round, but that doesn't matter. The important thing is that we get up there.'

'You're not leaving today?' There was alarm in Hannah's voice now. 'It will be dark soon.'

It was Alec Gilmore who answered. He'd taken the phone from her mother and was sounding very much in charge. 'We'll set out first thing in the morning when the roads shouldn't be too busy. With a bit of luck we should see you just after lunchtime.'

'You will drive carefully, Dad, won't you?'

Her father gave an indignant little cough at the other end of the phone. 'And when did I ever drive any other way?'

Jamie was tugging at Hannah's arm. 'Are Granny and Gramps coming to see us?' His blue eyes were shining.

She reached out and drew him close, smiling. 'Only if you and the others are very well behaved.'

Jamie gave a whoop and did a little dance before racing off to tell Robbie and Holly the news.

Hannah had invited Ross and Josh to join them for lunch. She'd just put the casserole in the oven when the Land Rover pulled into the yard. Her heart skipped a beat as she watched the pair of them make their way to the back door. 'It's open!' she called, racing to the kitchen mirror to pat down her wayward hair. She seldom wore make-up, but now, arching a dark brow at the glowing pink cheeks, she wished she had taken more care with her appearance that morning.

Ross's wide shoulders filled the small cottage doorway as he came in, carrying a big cardboard box. He nudged his son ahead of him into the room and gave Hannah a guilty smile. 'You always seem to be feeding us. I have a fully stocked larder back at the lodge, so I hope you will accept this.' He put the box on the table. 'It's just a bit of venison, and some things from the vegetable garden at the Big House.'

Hannah's hand went to her hot cheek as she stared at the contents of the box. They'd never dined out on anything this grand in the Maxwell household before. 'You didn't have to . . . ' she started, flustered.

'The venison was the laird's idea. He brought it over last night, so I can't take all the credit.'

Josh was wrinkling his nose, sniffing

at the delicious aromas coming from the oven. 'I'm glad we didn't stay at the lodge, Dad. I like coming here to Robbie and Jamie's house.'

Two of the puppies padded into the kitchen and, seeing Josh, bounded towards him. He gathered both of them up in his arms.

'The others are all through in the sitting room playing a board game,' Hannah told him. 'Why don't you go and join them?' They heard a chorus of greetings as the boy, still clutching both puppies, reached the other room.

Hannah moved to lift the box, but Ross put a hand on her arm. 'Allow me,' he said, smiling down at her.

That lightening bolt of connection surged through her again, and she took an involuntary step back, almost colliding with a chair.

He slid the box back onto the table and, turning, took Hannah by the shoulders and sat her in the chair. 'You're still all shaken up after the other day.' He took her hand. 'You're trembling, Hannah.

All this drama over the boys has really taken it out of you.' He put his hand on her forehead, his green eyes full of concern. 'I think you might have a temperature.'

Hannah was struggling to keep control of her emotions. She had a temperature all right, but she suspected it had more to do with the touch of Ross's fingers on her brow than any delayed reaction from their sons' little escapade. She took a deep breath and stood up. 'I'm fine, really I am.' She was back in control. 'But if you really want to help you could put that box of venison in the cold larder, then help me to set out the plates.'

'Granny and Gramps are coming up today,' Jamie announced as they later sat round the table. Ross raised an eyebrow and Hannah nodded.

'I know. I tried to persuade them to wait until the weather was better . . .' Her voice trailed off and she laughed. 'Maybe I didn't try too hard.'

Ross helped himself to a chunk of bread and mopped up the last of his gravy. 'No, you're right to want them here. Families are important.' There was a distant look in his eyes, and Hannah wondered if his own parents were still alive.

As usual, Ross insisted on helping with the washing up, which left Hannah with no more chores to do after they'd gone. She spent the next hour casting anxious glances to the lane for the first sight of her parents' little Mini. When it eventually appeared, she ran to the door. 'Oh you poor things, you look half frozen.'

'Well, where are they?' Peggy raised her voice so the children in the other room would hear. 'Where are those two little monkeys who go off into the wilderness and get themselves lost?'

Robbie and Jamie looked up sheepishly; and then, realising she was teasing, hurled themselves into Peggy's arms. She hugged them tight, burying her face in each head of floppy hair in turn. Hannah saw her blink away tears.

Peggy sniffed. 'Now come and tell me

what you two little scamps thought you were up to.'

Alec followed his wife into the room, giving Hannah's shoulders a squeeze as he passed. Holly took his hand and turned her huge blue eyes on him. 'Can I tell you what I've been up to, Gramps?'

Alec eased himself into an armchair and pulled Holly onto his knee. 'You certainly can, my angel.'

Hannah watched her little family, a lump in her throat, and wished she could always be as happy as she was right at that moment.

Half an hour later they were all seated round the kitchen table again, the children watching as Peggy and Alec tucked into the casserole Hannah had saved for them.

'This is delicious, Hannah. You must give me the recipe.'

'Don't embarrass me, Mum. You know it's just something I threw together. You were always the cook in the family.' She frowned. 'And speaking of cook . . . who's making all those school dinners at Logair Primary tomorrow?'

Peggy waved her knife. 'It's all in hand, love. My assistant cook Betty Ogilvie's taking over.' She smiled. 'And not just for tomorrow. I've taken some leave due to me and I've told them I won't be back until after the Christmas holidays.'

'What!' Hannah's eyes flew open. 'Can you do that, Mum?'

Peggy shrugged. 'I've done it.'

'But don't you worry, lass.' Alec placed his knife and fork together on his empty plate. 'We'll find a B&B somewhere. We're not planning to throw you out of your bed for two weeks.'

'You'll do no such thing.' Hannah's head was whirring, working out temporary sleeping arrangements. 'I can go in with Holly. It's not a problem.'

Holly's face lit up. 'You're coming to sleep in my bed, Mummy?' Her voice rose in disbelief. 'Really . . . ?'

Hannah nodded, laughing. 'Yes, really.'

After breakfast next morning, Alec offered to run the children to school.

'And we can collect them at home time,' Peggy offered.

Hannah looked up from the sink. 'You don't have to do that.' But Robbie, Jamie and Holly were nodding enthusiastically.

'We'd like to,' Peggy said. 'And, besides, it will give us a chance to see their school and maybe meet some of their new friends.'

'Can they, Mummy? Can Granny and Gramps take us to school?' Jamie pleaded.

Hannah frowned. 'The roads are still pretty snowy.'

Alec shook his head, shrugging. 'I have been driving buses around Glasgow for the past ten years, remember?'

'I know that, Dad. It's just . . . '

'We'll be careful, love. Promise.' Peggy turned to her grandchildren. 'Now, have you all got your satchels?'

'Rucksacks, Granny,' Robbie corrected. 'And yes, there're here.' He heaved a bright red bag over his shoulder and trouped after them.

Hannah followed them out and helped maneuver the children's car seats into her parents' small car. 'It's a bit of a squeeze,' she said, narrowing her eyes as they all clambered in. 'Ring me when you arrive. I'll be at the shop today.'

Her father tooted the horn, and they all waved as they took off up snowy the lane.

She was about to turn back to the cottage when a movement at the top of the lane caught her eye. A vehicle had been parked up on the top road, and was now moving off in the opposite direction. She could just make out its big dark shape as it passed beyond the trees. Had someone been watching the croft? She shook her head and dismissed the thought. It was ridiculous. More likely, some motorist had stopped to answer a mobile phone call. By the time she reached the post office in Corrieglen she'd forgotten all about it.

'It's great that your folks are here,' Maggie said as Hannah hung her coat up in the back shop. 'Have you recovered from all that excitement yet?'

'I haven't thanked you properly for what you did on Friday, Maggie. I don't think I would have got through that day without your support.'

Maggie coloured at the compliment, but waved a hand of dismissal. 'It's what friends are for. The important thing is that it all turned out so well.' She glanced out of the window at the crisp snow. 'It's a pretty picture now that it has all settled down. But nobody likes a blizzard, not even up here.' She turned back to Hannah. 'Anyway, the main thing is that no harm was done, and now it's my turn to be grateful to you. I really appreciate you coming in this morning, Hannah. We're always busy in the run-up to Christmas.'

Hannah glanced at the strings of tinsel festooning the shelves and the tiny decorated tree on the post office counter. 'It's only two weeks away and I haven't given it a thought,' she said dismally.

'You mean you haven't ordered a tree

yet?' Maggie was shocked.

Hannah shook her head. 'So much has happened over the past few weeks that I feel my feet have hardly touched the ground.'

'Well it's time they did, lassie,' Maggie scolded. 'You need to make a list.' She looked at her over her spectacles. 'Did you bring decorations from your old place?'

Hannah frowned. 'I think there's a box out in the shed, and an old artificial tree.'

Maggie's mouth fell open. 'There's a whole mountainside of young spruce trees out there and you're talking about artificial ones. That's sacrilege. Leave it with me. I'll sort something out.'

'Honestly, Maggie. You've done so much for us already. Our old tree will be fine.'

They both looked up as the bell on the shop door tinkled and the first customer of the day came in. 'Jess! We don't often see you in here.' Maggie forced a smile.

'Well, I haven't come to collect any benefit money, if that's what you're thinking. Gil's got himself a job over at Clayloan Farm, in the turkey processing shed.' She glanced at Hannah. 'We've run out of a few things up at the Big House. I don't suppose you have any liver pâté.'

Hannah smiled, indicating the cold cabinet. 'We do, as it happens.'

Another customer came in and began browsing through the shelves.

'I hear your boys got into a bit of trouble the other day.' Jess sniffed. 'They need teaching a lesson if you ask me.'

'I think they learned a pretty good lesson, but they're fine now. Thanks for asking,' Hannah said curtly. 'Will there be anything else?'

The woman slapped a five-pound note onto the counter and, after receiving her change, left without another word. Hannah stared after her, wondering why a nice man like the old laird would employ such an unpleasant woman.

The shop and post office were busy

all morning, and it was lunchtime before the subject of Jess Guthrie came up again. 'What's that woman's problem?' Hannah asked as Maggie brewed a pot of tea and broke open a new packet of chocolate digestives.

'You'd be well advised to stay clear of her.'

Hannah chewed her bottom lip. 'She really doesn't like me, does she?'

'She's jealous. She still thinks that layabout son of hers should have got the tenancy of Lanrig. She'll get over it.'

But Hannah wasn't so sure. Maggie didn't know about the brooch incident, when the Guthries had tried to pin the blame of its disappearance on her — and then this latest business of the missing necklace. And if this morning's exchange was anything to go by, the woman was still holding a grudge.

'Why does Sir John keep her on? As far as I could see she doesn't even treat him with much respect.'

Maggie shrugged. 'Changes don't

happen easily up here in the Highlands. I suppose the laird's just got used to Jess's ways.'

'But she doesn't live in the Big House?'

'Oh no, she and Duncan have a cottage on the other side of the village. The laird employs him as a handyman-cum-gardener.'

Hannah thought of the box of venison and fresh vegetables Ross had brought yesterday and wondered if they were a result of Duncan's handiwork. 'Is he a good gardener?'

'He can dig a vegetable patch and plant a few roses, nothing that any of the rest of us couldn't do if we put our minds to it. But it's like I said, the laird doesn't like change, so the Guthries stay.' She shrugged. 'I can't see them shifting, not when they have such a cushy number up there.'

The afternoon rush had begun to subside when Hannah glanced at the clock. It was almost three. Peggy had rung, saying they were already outside the school gates and waiting for the children.

'You get off now, Hannah. I can manage. You and your parents have a lot of catching up to do.'

'Are you sure, Maggie?'

Maggie disappeared into the back shop and came out dangling Hannah's coat. 'Put it on and get yourself home.'

Hannah grinned and did as she was told. 'I'll be back in the morning,' she called as she went out.

There was a strange feeling of unease in the pit of her stomach as she turned into the lane. Her parents' Mini wasn't in the yard. She checked her watch. Three-forty p.m. They should be home by now. Maybe the school was late in getting out. She took out her phone and punched in her mother's mobile number. It rang out, but there was no reply. An icy fear was beginning to grip her insides. Where were they?

With trembling fingers she tapped in Ross's number. He answered immediately.

'My folks haven't got back with the children yet, Ross. Are any of the roads up there blocked by snow?'

'The roads are fine. I was talking to Peggy and Alec before the school got out. There isn't a problem, Hannah. They're probably coming down the lane right now.'

Hannah glanced out. There was no sign of the cream Mini. 'I'm worried, Ross. They should have been home by now.'

'You stay there and let me know when they turn up. I'll have a cruise around in case they've stopped off somewhere.'

'Thank you, Ross. I'd appreciate that.'

It was half an hour before he found them. He'd almost missed the light-coloured Mini, as it lay balanced on two wheels in a ditch. The driver's door opened and Alec Gilmore climbed out, his face as white as the surrounding fields.

'Is everyone all right?' Ross yelled, racing towards them. One of the back doors creaked open and Peggy scrambled out, followed by Robbie and then Jamie. Holly was still in her car seat in the back. Ross could hear her begin to sob.

'We're all a bit wobbly, but we're fine,' Alec said, putting an arm around the two boys.

'Can you help Holly out?' Peggy's voice trembled.

'Take everybody back to the Land Rover, Alec,' Ross instructed. 'Leave Holly to me.' His fingers shook as he unbuckled the car seat and lifted the whimpering girl clear. 'My now, what an adventure you've all had,' he said, forcing a jovial note into his voice as he settled all of them in the warm vehicle. His hands were still trembling as he pulled the mobile from his pocket to call Hannah.

She'd made a grab for the phone the second it began to ring. 'Ross! Have you found them?'

'I have, and they're all safe and well. We'll be with you in about fifteen minutes.'

'Oh, thank God.' He could hear the

relief in her voice. 'What happened?'

Ross glanced at Alec. He was still shaking. 'They had a minor mishap on the road. They'll tell you all about it when we get back.' He glanced at the row of frightened little faces in his mirror. 'Might be an idea to stick the kettle on, Hannah. I think everyone could do with a nice big mug of hot chocolate.'

14

The dogs gave their usual welcome, scuttling excitedly around everyone's feet as they came into the kitchen. Hannah threw her arms around the children. 'You're all frozen,' she fussed, rubbing each pair of little hands in turn. She glanced at her parents, looking from one to the other, and was shocked to see how pale her father was. 'Are you two all right?'

'We're fine, love,' her mother said, coming forward to help Holly out of her coat.

Robbie's eyes lit up at the sight of the tray of hot chocolate and biscuits. 'Are these for us?'

Hannah nodded. 'Come through to the sitting room. It's nice and warm in there.'

Only when the three of them were settled on the carpet, with Tess and the puppies cuddling around them, did Hannah relax.

'When's tea, Mum?' Jamie called after her as she left the room.

'Soon, sweetheart.' She smiled back. 'I just want to have a word with Granny and Gramps first.'

Ross had found the sherry bottle and was pouring large measures for Hannah's parents.

'Now,' she said, joining them at the table, 'would somebody care to tell me what happened?'

'The car came off the road,' Peggy explained. 'With the Mini being almost white, I suppose the other driver didn't see us.' She sighed and took a sip from her glass. 'That's probably why he didn't stop.'

Hannah's eyes met Ross's. 'A car drove you off the road and the driver didn't stop?' She could hear her voice rising.

Her father lifted his glass and finished the sherry in two gulps before looking up, his eyes glinting with anger.

'He saw us all right.' His lips pressed together in a hard line. 'He saw us, and he drove straight for us!'

They all stared at him.

'That was no accident. Alec's face was grim. 'The man tried to kill us!'

Hannah sat in wide-eyed disbelief as her father told his story.

'Your mother gives everybody the benefit of the doubt.' He looked up and held his wife's gaze. 'It wasn't an accident, love. You know it wasn't.'

Peggy nodded miserably. Her voice came out in a croak. 'It was awful, Hannah. I thought we were all going to die.'

Ross's brow furrowed. 'Could you describe this vehicle?'

Alec shrugged. 'Only that it was a big black van. The driver was young . . . ' He shivered. 'I can still see him staring at me as he passed.' He caught the look that passed between Hannah and Ross. 'You both know this man? Who is he?'

'We can't be sure. There's no proof that the person we're thinking of is the one who ran you off the road. It's just that . . . ' Hannah clicked her fingers and sat up. 'I remember now. There was a vehicle sitting in the trees at the top of the lane when you drove off with the children this morning, Dad. I assumed it was someone who'd stopped to answer a call on his mobile phone.' She paused. 'He drove off in the other direction.'

'But?' Ross sat forward in his chair.

'But it was a big, dark vehicle!'

'I think we should call the police,' Peggy said.

Alec sighed. 'It would be this other driver's word against ours, love. And like you said, he'd probably claim not to have seen the cream Mini in the snow.'

'Except we know differently,' Ross said grimly.

Hannah met his eyes. 'What can we do, Ross? We can't just leave it like this.'

Ross checked his watch, getting to his feet. 'I have to go back to Corrieglen House to collect Josh. The Guthries should still be there. Let's see how they react when I tell them what's happened.'

Hannah got up. 'I'm coming with you.' She turned to Peggy and Alec. 'You don't mind looking after the children 'til I get back?'

Peggy shooed her off, rising from the table. 'Of course not. We'll get tea started.'

Hannah gave her mother a grateful smile. 'Thanks, Mum . . . Dad,' she called back as she hurried after Ross.

Her heart was pounding as the Land Rover's tyres crunched the hard-packed snow. 'Maggie warned me about this family. I should have listened to her.'

Ross glanced at her angry profile. 'Hold your horses, Hannah. We don't know for sure that it was Gil Guthrie driving that vehicle.'

'Oh, don't we? How many big black vans are there in Corrieglen?'

'OK, but let me do the talking when we get there.'

Hannah stared rigidly ahead. She was in no doubt now that Gil Guthrie had been the rogue driver. And if he was waiting for them at the Big House, there would be nothing Ross could do to stop her strangling the man with her bare hands.

The Land Rover hurtled up the drive to Corrieglen House, its wheels squealing to a halt as Ross rammed on the brakes. Together they stormed up the steps and threw open the front door. Ross was striding across the hall, with Hannah close behind, when Jess Guthrie came scurrying from the direction of the kitchen. She stopped dead when she saw them, too late to disguise the look of fear in her eyes.

She knew!

Hannah turned, glaring at the woman. 'Where's your son?'

The housekeeper looked flustered. 'He's not here.'

Ross stepped forward. 'Where can we find him?'

Jess swallowed. There was none of the bluster and bravado she had shown earlier when she'd spoken to Hannah in the shop. The panic in the beady black eyes was unmistakable.

Hannah spoke each word with cold disgust. 'My — children — could — have — died — today!'

Jess Guthrie took a step back. 'I don't know what you're talking about.' But her voice was hesitant, and her glance towards the kitchen told Hannah all she wanted to know. Gil Guthrie was in there!

Hannah turned to rush in, but Ross caught her arm. 'Easy, Hannah. Let me deal with this.'

No one heard the study door quietly open, and Josh and Sir John, his black Labrador by his side, approach. 'If there's something to be dealt with in my house, then I'll do the dealing,' the laird said.

Ross and Hannah swung round. Hannah's face coloured. 'I'm so sorry, Sir John. We were on our way to see you . . . ' She held out her hand to Josh, and he came forward to take it.

Ross ruffled his son's hair. 'Have you been behaving yourself?'

The boy nodded and pointed to the laird's dog. 'Moby's been helping me to build a snow castle.'

The laird pursed his lips and looked down at Josh. 'He brings new life to this old place.' He gave the boy a crooked grin. 'We're friends, aren't we, Josh?' Josh nodded.

The laird indicated one of the paneled doors. 'There's a television set in there. I'll get someone to bring you some juice and biscuits while I have a little talk with your father.'

'Can Moby come with me?' Josh asked hopefully.

Sir John glanced at the old dog, which thumped his tail on the floor.

'I don't see why not. Off you both go.'

'We'll just be another few minutes, Josh,' Ross called after his son, as he headed off with the big dog in search of the TV.

'Well now, what's all this about?' Sir John said. 'And where were you all going when I came out just now?'

The distraction had given Jess time to

compose herself. She folded her arms across her ample chest. 'I've no idea, sir. You'll have to ask them.'

Hannah glared at her. The woman was going to brazen it out. She'd no doubt that Gil, having heard the commotion in the hall, would now have scarpered, like the coward he undoubtedly was.

Ross had obviously come to the same conclusion, for he suggested they all return to the laird's study. Jess followed them to the door, but Ross's arm came out to bar her way.

'I don't think we'll need you in here, Mrs Guthrie,' he said coldly.

Hannah saw the flash of anger in the housekeeper's eye, but she raised no objection. She turned on her heel and marched briskly back across the hall.

Sir John took a pipe from his pocket and began to fill the bowl with tobacco, pushing it down before igniting it. Hannah could see the bowl glowing as drew up the smoke. He looked from one to the other, a questioning smile on his lips.

'Well now, who's going first?'

Ross cleared his throat and began. Hannah watched the laird's expression turn from disbelief to astonishment as Ross described the afternoon's events. He sat down heavily in the chair behind his desk.

'And you believe Mrs Guthrie's son was responsible?'

They both nodded. 'The description Hannah's father gave of the vehicle that ran them off the road fits Gil's black van perfectly.'

'Then we must call the police,' Sir John said.

'We thought we would give him the benefit of the doubt first, sir,' Ross explained. 'Mrs Guthrie said he wasn't here, but we were on our way to the kitchen to check that when you arrived.'

Sir John took another puff on his pipe. 'She told you her son wasn't here, did she?' He paused, pondering this. 'But I saw his old van coming up the drive about an hour before you turned up.'

Hannah met Ross's eyes. His expression was grim.

The laird's brow furrowed. 'I don't like my staff telling lies. Is there anything else I should know?'

Ross looked at Hannah, his eyes serious. She nodded. 'Tell him, Ross. Tell him everything. It's about time the laird knew what's been going on under his own roof.'

The first thing Hannah saw when Ross dropped her off at the croft was the big Christmas tree propped up against the back door.

'Maggie!' She grinned. 'She said Jake would find us a tree. I just wasn't expecting one this big.'

Ross cocked his head, studying her with a slow smile. 'You see . . . we're not all bad people in Corrieglen. I don't think the Guthries will be bothering you again.'

She leaned across and kissed his cheek. 'Thank you, Ross,' she whispered.

He caught her hand, his eyes studying her face in the darkness. 'You have nothing to thank me for.'

She kissed the tips of his fingers, and pressed them to her lips. 'Oh, yes I have,' she said softly, matching his gaze for a long few seconds before turning and jumping out of the Land Rover.

All the anguish and anger of earlier had vanished as she stood watching the vehicle's taillights move up the lane and turn out of view. Her family was safe — and she had a good man looking out for her. A tiny bud of happiness was beginning to burst deep inside her.

Peggy was clearing the table as Hannah walked into the kitchen. Her mother swung round, her eyes questioning. 'Well? Did you find that driver?'

Hannah put up a hand. 'Let me just check on the children and then I'll tell you and Dad everything.'

Robbie and Jamie were sprawled on the carpet, each of them reading a book. Holly was on her granddad's knee. She scrambled down and came running when she saw Hannah.

'I've got a surprise for everyone,'

Hannah said, putting a finger to her mouth. The boys sat up. Even Tess, who was stretched out in front of the fire with her sleeping pups, cocked a brow.

'It's outside.' She crooked her finger. 'Come and see.'

She threw open the back door to a chorus of gasps from behind her.

'It's a Christmas tree!' Holly danced out into the snow. 'Santa Claus has sent us a Christmas tree!'

'Wow,' Jamie said, his eyes wide.

Robbie put his fingers on the prickly branches. 'It's real,' he confirmed with a wide grin.

'It's lovely,' Peggy laughed. 'Do you think Mummy will let Gramps and I help you to decorate it tomorrow?'

They all looked at Hannah. She nodded, laughing. 'We can all decorate it.'

After the children were in bed, Hannah and her parents settled in front of the fire as she gave them a blow-by-blow account of what had happened at the Big House.

She looked up at her father. 'Did you

report it to the police, Dad?'

Alec nodded. 'I had to, for the sake of the insurance. They took a statement over the phone. I think they're treating it as a hit and run. Someone will call out to interview us properly in the morning. I also rang that recovery service Ross recommended. They're sending people to pull the car out of the ditch. We won't know how badly damaged it is until then.'

Hannah reached to touch her father's arm. 'I'm so sorry. You and Mum didn't deserve all this.'

Peggy smiled. 'Let's not despair just yet, love. The car might be fine. The really important thing is that none of us was hurt.'

'And that rascal, Guthrie, gets off scott-free,' Hannah muttered.

'Maybe not,' Alec said. 'I can identify him, remember.'

'But there's no proof, Dad. It's your word against his. And when push comes to shove, that unpleasant family of his will lie through their teeth to give him an alibi.' Hannah released a long, heartfelt sigh. 'The worst thing is, if he's still living around here, I could meet him on any street corner.'

A look of alarm flashed into Peggy's eyes. 'D'you think he still means your family harm?'

Hannah grimaced. 'It's Gil Guthrie who needs to worry. I won't be responsible for my actions the next time I come across him.'

Everyone was up early next morning. Hannah was treating them all to a cooked breakfast, and the appetising aroma of bacon grilling was permeating the cottage.

'I'm feeling really guilty about going off to help Maggie when you and Mum are here on your own,' Hannah said later, as Peggy helped the children struggle into their coats.

Alec Gilmore brushed aside his daughter's concern. 'The police should be here to take that statement any time now, and the garage has promised us a courtesy car. If it arrives in time, we might even drive to Dingwall to do some Christmas shopping.'

'Well, keep in touch, won't you,' Hannah called as she shepherded the children out the door.

Maggie knew something had happened as soon as Hannah walked into the shop. 'Gil Guthrie did what?' Her eyes widened in disbelief as Hannah recounted the story.

'I knew he was a bad lot, but I never imagined he would do anything as awful as that.' She clapped her hands to her cheeks. 'Are the children all right?'

Hannah nodded. 'They're fine. But Mum and Dad were a bit shaken up. They tried to hide it, but I could tell.'

Maggie shook her head.

'Poor Peggy and Alec. What a horrible thing to happen.'

Hannah began straightening up the tins of salmon. 'Jess is backing her son to the hilt, of course. She was so defensive when Ross and I went up to Corrieglen House last night. I'm sure Gil was in the kitchen, and made off when he heard our voices.'

The first customers began arriving as soon as Maggie flicked the 'open' sign around. Their shopping lists were not long, as most people did their main shop at the supermarket in Glenburn, or drove to Dingwall. So Hannah wasn't exactly rushed off her feet, but the lunch break had lasted only ten minutes when the shop bell began to tinkle again. She looked up and was surprised to see Ross going round the shelves. His head jerked round and he grinned, raising his basket.

'Just a few standbys. Josh is eating me out of house and home.'

Hannah smoothed down her blue apron. 'Boys have healthy appetites.'

He stopped, narrowing his eyes, as though deciding whether or not to share something with her. 'Can I drop by later, Hannah? There's something you should know.'

'I've a better idea,' she said. 'You and Josh come for tea. I'll collect him from school when I fetch my three.' After

Ross left, Hannah spent the rest of the afternoon wondering what it was he had to tell her.

She got the usual exuberant welcome from Tess and her pups after school, when she and the children burst into the kitchen.

'Hello, darlings. Have you all had a nice day?' Peggy called, getting up from her armchair in the sitting room and coming through to greet them.

Alec appeared from behind her. 'We've got an old Ford Fiesta to run around in until the Mini's fixed.'

'We saw it in the yard,' Hannah said. 'At least you're mobile.'

He came forward and kissed his daughter on the cheek. 'It would seem that the Guthrie lad has done a runner. The police went to the family's cottage to talk to him, but his parents claimed not to have seen him for days.'

Hannah grimaced. 'Well that's not true. Still, if Gil's disappeared, then at least I don't have to worry about seeing him around here.' She glanced to her mother. 'Did you go to Dingwall?'

Peggy had a glint in her eye. 'We've been too busy for that. Come and see.' She grabbed Hannah's hand and began pulling her towards the sitting room.

But the surprise had already been discovered, judging by the whoops of delight she could hear.

'Voila,' Peggy said, making a gesture towards the Christmas tree, which now sat upright in a wooden trough. 'Dad made it. What d'you think? All it needs now are some lights and decorations.'

Hannah clamped her hands around her cheeks. 'It's brilliant, Dad. Thank you.'

Alec Gilmore's face was pink with pleasure. 'I dug out this box of tree decorations from the shed.' He pulled a tattered cardboard box from behind a chair. 'There weren't nearly enough for this big tree, so I popped over to Glenburn and bought a few more, and a couple of extra sets of lights.' He stood back, admiring the tree. 'The rest is up to you, children.'

More whoops of delight. 'Can we start now, Mummy?' Holly coaxed.

'I don't see why not,' Hannah laughed.

It was easy to make the macaroni cheese dish she had planned stretch to another two portions. It was bubbling nicely in the oven by the time Ross arrived. Josh raced out and pulled his father in to the sitting room to see the newly decorated tree.

'My, you have been busy,' Ross said. 'Maybe you can all come over to the lodge and help Josh decorate our tree.'

Josh's eyes flew wide. 'Have you bought us a Christmas tree, Dad?'

'I certainly have.' He beamed around the room. 'And you're all invited to tea at our place on Friday night.'

He followed Hannah back to the kitchen. 'I have some news,' he said. 'Maybe you'd like to sit down before I tell you.'

She wrinkled her nose. 'It's nothing bad, is it?'

Ross shook his head. 'Quite the opposite. Sir John has sacked the Guthries.'

Hannah's mouth fell open.

'Told them to pack their things and get out. He's severed their tenancy agreement as well.'

Peggy had walked in and was staring at Ross. 'Did I hear right? Are the Guthries really going?'

Ross nodded. 'Absolutely.'

Peggy put an arm around her daughter. 'Well, about time too, if what Hannah told us is right.'

'That's the good news,' Ross said. 'The bad news is that Sir John will have to cancel the traditional estate dinner. It's held every year in the week before Christmas.' He shook his head. 'It's such a shame because all the food's been ordered, but the laird has no one to cook it.'

'What's involved in this dinner? I mean . . . is it a banquet?' Peggy asked.

'It's a big traditional Christmas dinner for about forty people,' Ross said.

Hannah glanced at her mother, and then put up her hand. 'Wait a minute,

Mum. You're not thinking of volunteer-ing, are you?'

Peggy lifted her chin. 'That all depends on whether or not I like this old laird of yours.'

15

'You really think you could cook a Christmas dinner for so many people?' The laird fixed Peggy with an uncertain stare. Ross had driven her to Corrieglen House to meet him.

Peggy's chin came up in a defiant tilt. 'I don't see why not. I cook for far more than that every day.'

'I told you she was a capable lady.' Ross grinned.

Sir John came round from behind his desk and took Peggy's hand. 'My dear lady, if you can do this for me, I will be eternally grateful.'

'Nonsense.' Peggy coloured. 'Just point me in the direction of the kitchen.'

Sir John and Ross led the way, with Peggy quickening her step to keep up with them. They crossed the vast hall, where portraits of the laird's ancestors looked down on them from their gilt frames. Sir John threw open a door at the end of a long corridor to reveal a kitchen that could have come straight from the dark ages.

Peggy gasped. Heavy oak cupboards lined the walls, and tea towels that looked none too clean to her critical eye dangled untidily from an overhead wooden pulley. She took in the vast ceramic sinks, too deep to be practical for modern use, and the large, rattling windows stretching from the worktops to the high ceiling.

Sir John saw Peggy wince at the ancient black range. Glancing at Ross, he shifted his weight uneasily from one slippered foot to the other. 'There's an electric cooker as well,' he explained, indicating the small stainless steel oven and hob in the far corner. 'I think Mrs Guthrie mostly used that.'

The laird waited for Peggy to say something, but she was silent, her eyes roaming the room.

He sighed. 'You're right; it's not very

modern, is it? I will completely understand if you've changed your mind about taking on our function.'

Peggy thought of her gleaming school kitchen, with its fridges, deep freeze, and industrial-sized ovens, and squared her shoulders. 'Well it's not what I'm used to,' she admitted. 'But I never turn down a challenge, so if you still want me to cook for your Christmas function . . . '

Sur John didn't give her a chance to finish the sentence. He'd grasped her hand and was pumping it in gratitude. 'I believe Mrs Guthrie has already ordered the food. There should be a list somewhere . . . ' His gaze wandered over the room.

Peggy put a hand on his arm. 'It's fine, Sir John. Just leave it all to me now.' She waited until the door closed behind him before turning to Ross. 'How many did he say this dinner was for?'

Ross narrowed his eyes, but he was smiling. 'You wouldn't be chickening out, would you?'

'Oh no, I'll see this through. But you'll have to help me.' She fished in her bag for the notebook and pen she'd brought and for the next half hour they sat at the big wooden table, Peggy scribbling down the details of the shops, suppliers and telephone numbers of all the food and drink suppliers Corrieglen House dealt with.

'I think Jess Guthrie ordered most of the food, but you'll have to check,' Ross said.

Peggy went round the cupboards, checking the contents and making notes of what extra cutlery and tableware they might need.

'What about staff? I'll need some people to help in the kitchen, and also to serve the food.'

Ross nodded. 'No problem. I'll put a list of names together.'

Peggy blew out her cheeks as she went over her plans in her mind. 'Thank goodness I have a daughter who can cook.'

Ross spun round, his face falling. 'You want Hannah to help you in the kitchen?' He couldn't keep the disappointment out of his voice.

Peggy raised an eyebrow. 'You don't think I should ask her?'

He cleared his throat. 'Actually, Peggy . . . I . . . I was hoping that Hannah would be my guest at the dinner.'

Peggy's eyes widened. Ross and her daughter? She hadn't been expecting that. But why not? He was always at the house . . . and she had, more than once, caught that look that passed between them. This day was turning out better than she had expected.

She smiled. 'I think that's a much better idea, Ross. Hannah deserves a night out.'

After he left, Peggy wandered around the kitchen. An old laundry room she hadn't noticed earlier had been turned into a utility space and housed a tall fridge freezer stocked with ready meals. She picked one up and dropped it back, shaking her head. Was this what the laird's housekeeper had been feeding him? He deserved better than that.

Peggy slipped off her coat and rolled up her sleeves. An hour later she was sliding the chicken pie she had made out of the oven and sliding in a jam sponge. The meal might be simple, but it was wholesome — and the old man looked like he needed feeding up.

Peggy brushed aside the laird's gratitude as she placed the home-cooked meal before him. 'Call it a bit of practice,' she told him, laughing.

There was a spring in her step as she headed for her car. She was smiling. Hannah and Ross . . . the names even sounded right together!

She had promised Hannah that she would call by the shop on her way home to tell her how the meeting with the laird had gone and was amused to find that she and Maggie had been looking out for her. They crowded into the back room to listen with growing mirth to Peggy's account of Corrieglen House's ancient kitchen.

Maggie shook her head. 'I don't suppose an old bachelor like Sir John ever gave much thought to modernising the place. I doubt if he's even been in it all that often.'

Peggy giggled. 'Oh it's not that bad. We'll just have to work around the problems.'

Hannah traced a finger around the rim of her coffee mug. 'Was Ross there?'

Peggy looked up and smiled as Hannah glanced quickly away. 'He was, and he was very helpful.' She described the lists they'd compiled together, the telephone numbers he'd given her, and the contacts that would give the best deals.

Hannah nodded. 'I don't know what that estate would do without Ross. He's a different man these days. I suppose it's having Josh back living with him that's put the smile on his face.' She knew they were both looking at her. If she blushed now, she would give away her feelings. The shop door tinkled and she jumped up. 'I'd better see to that.'

'Are you sure you want to do this, Mum?' Hannah asked later, as Peggy sat in the croft kitchen poring over the notes she'd made. 'You and Dad are supposed to be on holiday, and here you both are up to your eyes in organising the catering for a Highland estate's Christmas banquet. I feel really guilty not helping you.'

She still couldn't quite believe that Ross had invited her to accompany him.

Peggy slid off her specs and waved her notebook in the air. 'I have all the help I need right here. Most of them are village women whom I've already met and can trust. The food's been delivered, and the table in that long banqueting hall has been dressed and set. All you have to do is to turn up on Ross's arm looking beautiful.'

Hannah's cheeks burned. 'Ross and I are just friends. You do know that, don't you, Mum?'

They were friends, but that didn't stop Hannah's heart turning over like a lovesick teenager's every time she saw him. She tried to think back to how she'd felt when she first met Brian. She thought she'd loved him, but it had never been anything like this. She'd never felt giddy with excitement when he walked into a room, hadn't felt a wave of pleasure when he spoke her name ... and she'd certainly never trembled when Brian touched her.

That night Hannah stared into the darkness as Holly snuggled close to her. She could never let Ross suspect how she really felt. The last thing she wanted was to scare him off. Their time together was precious, but if friendship was all there would ever be between them, then she would settle for that.

Peggy and Alec set off early on the morning of the estate function. And for the umpteenth time Hannah went to the wardrobe to check on the long, dark green silk dress she had made herself. She'd bought the material on a whim in Glasgow months before they moved to Lanrig. Until now, she had found no use for it. Today, it hung in luxurious folds from its hanger. The green tartan sash, made from a remnant she'd found in her box of left over fabrics, added an extra touch of glamour.

Maggie offered to babysit, so Hannah had suggested to Ross that Josh should come for a sleepover.

She hadn't meant to make an entrance that evening, but that was exactly what she did. Maggie had been reading a story to the four children in the sitting room, Ross laughing with them over her shoulder. They all turned as she walked in.

This was a Hannah none of them had seen before, and the children stared at her wide-eyed.

Holly scrambled up and danced around her. 'You look just like a beautiful lady.'

'Well, thank you, my darling,' Hannah laughed, not daring to glance at Ross. 'But you don't have to sound so surprised.'

Robbie got to his feet. 'Holly's right, Mum. You're beautiful.' Jamie nodded enthusiastically.

Maggie smiled. 'I'll second that.'

Only Ross was silent. And when she summed up the courage to look at him, her knees almost turned to jelly. She had to stifle a gasp at how handsome he looked in a kilt. Hannah recognised the rich green Hunter tartan. She took in the black Prince Charlie jacket and waistcoat with their silver buttons all bearing the emblem of the thistle. It looked as though he had taken as much care over his appearance tonight as she had.

She saw him swallow, his eyes never leaving her face. Had she overdone things with such a glamorous dress? . . . Were the sparkly slides she'd used to pin back her long, dark hair just a touch too much?

Then he smiled, and she could see the undisguised delight in his eyes. 'You'll be the belle of the ball,' he said.

'Ball?' Hannah repeated, after he'd helped her into the Land Rover and he'd climbed into the driver's seat.

Ross nodded. 'Didn't I mention that?

It's nothing fancy, but Sir John always gets a couple of fiddlers to come along after the meal and we have a bit of a ceilidh . . . not that I've ever stuck around for it before.' He glanced at her in the darkness. 'But I think I'm going to enjoy it tonight.'

Hannah felt a shiver of excitement shoot through her body. 'What's different about tonight?' she asked softly.

He reached across to take her hand. 'You're here, Hannah. That's what's different.'

Her heart was beginning to thud as he raised her fingers and brushed them with his lips. She took a slow, shaky breath. 'Thank you for inviting me, Ross,' she said quietly.

The scene they met as they approached Corrieglen House made her gasp. A huge Christmas tree, bedecked with twinkling lights, had been erected to the left of the main door. On the other side, a kilted piper was filling the night air with his lilting music.

Sir John, in full Highland dress, came

to greet them as they entered. His eyes lit up when he saw Hannah, and he came forward to kiss her cheek. 'You look just beautiful, my dear. I hope you're saving a dance for me later.'

Hannah blushed. 'It would be my pleasure, Sir John.'

'Your mother has done us proud this evening. Just wait 'til you see the wonderful feast she has prepared.'

Hannah glanced up at Ross. 'I should just pop in to see her.'

'I would advise doing that a little later,' the laird said. 'It all looked pretty frantic in there last time I checked.'

'Sir John's right, Hannah. Let's just take out seats.'

Ross's popularity was obvious from the way people greeted him, some coming from the other side of the room to shake his hand. Even though Hannah didn't actually know them, she recognised most of the faces from seeing them around the village and in the shop. It was a good feeling, being part of the community.

The laird took his place at the head of the table, with Ross and Hannah on either side. Each delicious course was met with a murmur of compliments that made Hannah glow with pride for her mother's efforts.

'I really will have to see Mum now,' Hannah said, as they all rose from the table after the meal.

In the kitchen, Peggy and Alec had collapsed into chairs. She went to hug her mother. 'That dinner was amazing, Mum. What a triumph. I think they'll be falling over themselves out there to congratulate you.'

She saw their eyes widen and a look of amazement cross their faces as they took in her lovely gown and glowing cheeks.

'You look just beautiful, sweetheart,' Peggy said, making Hannah do a twirl.

'So you do, love,' her father echoed.

Hannah put her hands on her hips. 'I didn't come to talk about me. You should hear the praises for your cooking out there, Mum. You've both done a wonderful job tonight.'

Alec cocked his head. 'I think the music's starting. Ross will be wondering where you've disappeared to.'

Hannah laughed and kissed them both. 'I'd better get back.'

They watched her as she moved lightly along the corridor. Alec squeezed his wife's hand. 'Our lass is happy again, Peggy.'

Peggy nodded, choking back a sudden wave of emotion.

They listened as the lively notes of the fiddle music echoed through the old house.

'I think this family's reached a turning point,' Peggy said softly.

Hannah hadn't danced like this since she was a schoolgirl. Ross whirled her around the floor as the fiddle music grew louder and faster. 'Stop,' she laughed breathlessly. But he ignored her.

'You're not giving up on me now, are you?' he yelled over the thumping of feet in the 'Eightsome Reel'.

'Not me,' she called back, her dark

hair flying out as she skipped around the floor.

At last the music slowed, and couples moved into each other's arms for the last waltz. Ross held Hannah so close, she could feel the beat of his heart. His head nestled against hers, as she closed her eyes to the exquisite pleasure of the moment.

'Have you enjoyed yourself, Hannah?' he whispered in her ear as the tune ended.

She nodded, too full of emotion to speak. Ross took her silence for tiredness and guided her to the door.

'Don't be a stranger, Hannah,' the laird called after them as they turned for a final wave.

Peggy and Alec had slipped out earlier, after being satisfied that the kitchen was spick and span. They had plenty to think about tonight. Their courtesy car was by the back door, and the lights were still on in the croft when Ross and Hannah drove into the yard.

'I'd ask you in for a nightcap, but I'm

afraid it will have to be coffee.' Hannah gave Ross a crooked grin. 'We're right out of cooking sherry.'

Ross reached into the back and produced a bottle of champagne. 'It's just as well I came prepared, then.'

Peggy and Alec were waiting for them in the sitting room. Hannah ran upstairs to check on the children, and returned smiling. 'Out like lights, all four of them.'

'Is it all right if I go up to say goodnight to Josh?' Ross asked. Hannah nodded.

Peggy and Alec stood up. 'We have something to tell you, love,' her father began, looking at his wife. 'You tell her, Peggy.'

Peggy cleared her throat as Ross came back into the room. 'I'm glad you're both here. The thing is . . . well, the laird has offered your dad and me jobs.'

Hannah's eyes widened.

'He wants me to be his housekeeper, and Dad to look after the garden and be a general handyman.' Peggy smiled at them both. 'But the best part is . . . there's a cottage to go with it.'

Hannah gulped. 'Am I understanding this right? Sir John has offered you the Guthries' jobs?'

Ross's face had broken into a wide grin. Hannah was still staring at them, amazed. 'And have you accepted?'

They both nodded. 'We start after the New Year.' Peggy beamed.

'Oh, Mum . . . Dad!' Hannah flew across the room to hug them. 'This is wonderful!' She clasped her hands. 'You'll be living right here in Corrieglen.' She spun round to Ross, her eyes shining. 'Just wait 'til we tell the children.'

Neither of them saw the look that passed between Hannah's parents. Alec gave a little cough. 'We'll get off to bed now, love,' he said. 'We can talk everything over in the morning.'

'Don't go yet,' Hannah said. 'Ross has brought champagne.'

'Won't you join us for a nightcap?' Ross offered.

But Peggy and Alec shook their heads, smiling. 'We'll just go up if you don't mind,' Peggy said. 'It's been quite a day.'

Hannah watched them go and shook her head, smiling. She knew they were deliberately leaving her and Ross alone together.

If Ross had also suspected it, he showed no sign. He nodded towards the kitchen. 'I think your parents' news is worth toasting, even if they have left us to do it on their behalf. I'll pour us both a drink.'

Hannah smiled. She was certain now that there was a whole lot more than that to toast.

She was on the sofa, gazing into the flickering fire when he came back and put their glasses on the low table. They sat together, watching the flames curling over the glowing pine logs.

'It's been a wonderful evening, Hannah,' Ross said, his voice thick with emotion. 'I was so proud of you tonight.'

She turned to him. 'It was wonderful for me, too, Ross.'

He lifted her hand, kissing the tips of

each finger, before caressing her face. Hannah closed her eyes as his mouth came down on hers. The room spun around them, but the music she could hear was in her heart.

'Have you any idea how much I love you, my darling?' he murmured.

She traced the line of his jaw, feeling the muscles tense at her touch. 'Do you, Ross? Do you really love me?'

He tilted her chin until she was looking into his eyes. 'I want to marry you, Hannah. Will you marry me?'

She pulled back to stare at him. 'Are you sure that's what you want? I come with quite a big package.'

'If you mean those three great kids, then yes.' He smiled at her. 'I'm absolutely sure.'

Hannah choked back the lump in her throat. 'In that case . . . ' She stroked his cheek. 'There's nothing I would love more.'

He bent his head to kiss her again, but a creak on the stairs made them draw apart. A tousle-haired Josh appeared, rubbing bleary eyes.

'Is it morning, Daddy?' he asked in a sleepy voice. 'Have you come to collect me?'

Ross and Hannah looked at each other and dissolved into laughter. Hannah made to get up. 'I'll see to him.'

But Ross's hand came out to stop her. 'No, that's my job.'

Smiling down at Josh, he took his hand. Hannah could hear their voices all the way back up the stairs. She stretched luxuriously. Outside she could see the silver ribbon of water at the bottom of the pasture, and the sudden urge to share her happiness with the world was overwhelming.

Pulling on a wrap, she went out to Erin's pasture. Seeing her approach, the little horse moved closer, nuzzling Hannah's arm to have her mane stroked.

In the light from the full moon, the snowy pasture glistened like a field of diamonds. She held up her face to the night, and breathed in its magic.

She didn't hear Ross's silent approach.

His arms came around her. 'You'll catch cold.'

She smiled up at him. 'Not when I've got you to keep me warm.'

The sounds of the river reached them, murmuring whispers in the still of the night.

Ross nestled his cheek next to Hannah's. 'Lizzie had a special name for this spot.'

Hannah turned into his shoulder and raised an eyebrow.

'She used to call it the place where moonbeams dance.' His lips curved into a wistful smile.

'It's perfect,' she said softly, before he kissed her.

THE END

MORE THAN A PORTRAIT

Diana Dennison

When Jane is offered a job in northern Italy, with its promise of sunshine and colour, mountains and romantic scenery, her adventurous spirit can hardly refuse. Then she meets her employer: the unpredictable, pompous and dictatorial Duncan Frobisher. Sparks immediately fly between them, and Jane comes to know more than her fair share of elation and black depression before her temporary employment comes to an end . . .

FORGOTTEN

Fay Cunningham

Driving home in the dark, Serena stops to help an injured man lying in a ditch. He mutters something unintelligible, but that is only the start of her problems. Someone is watching the apartment she shares with her brother, her mother is being particularly secretive, and police detective Jack Armstrong is convinced Serena is hiding something. Just when she thinks things can get no worse, her missing father turns up. This is definitely not the time to fall in love.